A ROOM IN CHE

MICHAEL NELSON (known as 'Mickey'. _____ .... as a journalist before the Second World War, and during the war worked as secretary to John Lehmann, a prominent publisher and man of letters, and served as a captain in the Royal Army Service Corps. After his demobilisation, he lived with his boyfriend in Winchester and owned a bookstore there before meeting Rachel Holland, who knew he was gay but married him anyway; the two remained married the rest of their lives. Nelson and his wife relocated to London, where he was well known in the drinking establishments of Soho. Nelson's first novel, *Knock or Ring* (1957), which concerned the illegal practices of the 'ring', a group of booksellers who conspired to fix auctions and share profits among themselves, drew on his own experiences as a bookseller and received good reviews. His second book, *A Room in Chelsea Square* (1958), was published anonymously, and has gone on to become a gay classic. His other books are *Blanket* (1959) (published under the pseudonym 'Henry Stratton'), *When the Bed Broke* (1961), *Captain Blossom* (1973), *Captain Blossom Soldiers On* (1974), *Nobs & Snobs* (1976), *Captain Blossom in Civvy Street* (1978), and *Fear No More* (1989). Michael Nelson died in 1990.

GREGORY WOODS was Professor of Gay and Lesbian Studies at Nottingham Trent University until 2013. His main critical publications are *Articulate Flesh: Male Homo-eroticism and Modern Poetry* (1987) and *A History of Gay Literature: The Male Tradition* (1998), both from Yale University Press. His poetry, of which *An Ordinary Dog* (2011) was the most recent collection, is published by Carcanet Press. His website is www.gregorywoods.co.uk.

Cover: The cover has been adapted from Hans Tisdall's jacket design for the 1958 Jonathan Cape edition. Born in Germany in 1910, Tisdall entered the Academy of Fine Art in Munich in 1928 and in 1930 came to London, where he became well known for his textile designs, murals, and striking book jacket designs. Tisdall died in 1997.

A ROOM IN CHELSEA SQUARE

MICHAEL NELSON

With a new introduction by
GREGORY WOODS

VALANCOURT BOOKS

A Room in Chelsea Square by Michael Nelson
First published London: Jonathan Cape, 1958
First Valancourt Books edition 2014

Published by Valancourt Books, Richmond, Virginia
Publisher & Editor: JAMES D. JENKINS
20th Century Series Editor: SIMON STERN, University of Toronto
http://www.valancourtbooks.com

ISBN 978-1-939140-89-0 (*trade paperback*)
Also available as an electronic book.

Set in Dante MT 11/13.5

INTRODUCTION

A Room in Chelsea Square was first published anonymously in 1958. Its author was a charming but rather ineffectual young man called Michael Nelson (1921-1990). It is a book that excites very different responses. To some, it is a camp tour de force, full of wit and whimsy, a waspishly self-deprecating view of a certain type of homosexual circle from within its soulless heart or heartless soul. Some people find it very funny.

To others, especially in the decade or so after its first publication, it is a parade of negative representations of homosexual men, following many of the imposed, homophobic stereotypes of the age and ending with an obligatory, if somewhat peripheral, death. Falling into the hands of the isolated gay teenager, it was not likely to raise the spirits; it could not foster pride or solidarity. This is not a novel about what was then called the 'homosexual problem'. Nor is it about what so many publishers' blurbs used to refer to as 'the twilight world of the homosexual'.

It contains no social defence of same-sex love. In that regard, it is not what one would happily call a 'gay novel' at all. It has not a single attractive and sympathetic character with whom the gay reader can identify. There is no plea for tolerance, let alone acceptance. If any of these characters are meant to be representative, the book can add nothing to an argument in favour of law reform. Although they seem never to be having sex with each other (that has to be assumed between the lines, where plausible), these are far from being the discreet, well-behaved, consenting-adults-in-private envisaged by the Wolfenden Report (which, in 1957, recommended reform of the laws on homosexual acts in England and Wales). They socialise in public places and behave with ostentatious *sang froid*. If hidden at all, they are, like Poe's purloined letter, hidden in plain sight.

And yet, one might argue, it is the very lack of an affirmative or apologetic theme that is so impressive about it. Its main virtue is that it takes homosexuality completely for granted. There is anguish aplenty, but not about being gay. Most is about being unloved or unmoneyed. Perhaps that is the point: there are more important things to worry about—a poorly cooked meal, an ill-chosen tie—than the trivial matter of being queer.

Other than by reading the publisher's blurb, how does the reader first learn that the book's central characters are gay? The narrator never says this of them. We do hear that Patrick was sent down from his Oxford college for calling the Warden 'an old-fashioned suppressed quean'; but not until later in the book—and then only by inference—shall we realise that this is also a pretty accurate description of Patrick himself.

Only two words are ever used, throughout the book, to denote a homosexual man; and each is used only once. In the case just mentioned, Patrick uses 'quean' to insult an older man; and, much later, the newspaper editor Stuart Andrews refers to Ronnie Gras, mistakenly, as a 'pansy'. Never are any of the central homosexual characters explicitly referred to as such, either pejoratively or otherwise. Indeed, in the whole book, there is not a single explicitly positive reference to homosexuality at all.

One other pejorative term does come up, if only by the implication of its opposite. When Patrick suspects Nicholas of having brought a woman back to the flat in his absence, he contemptuously refers to him, and to others of his ilk, as 'you *normals*'. He is wrong about this: for, as far as we can tell, Nicholas is as much of an *abnormal* as Patrick himself. This crude terminology is ultimately derived from a discourse that was especially powerful in the 1940s and 1950s, that of the mental health industry. It was an era when the skills of parenting were policed with constant references to the 'normal' and the 'abnormal' child. Despite his sense of his own superiority to popular culture, Patrick has internalised this discourse and is apparently happy to spit it out at one he supposedly loves.

The date of publication (1958) places the book just after the Wolfenden Report (1957) recommended law reform (not to be achieved until a decade later). But this is misleading, since Nelson actually wrote it in the late 1940s. The early version was called *A Room in Russell Square* and its relationships were heterosexual (Patrick was an unlikely Patricia). One can see why it failed to find a publisher, lacking the unique selling point of its homosexual theme. The delay in publication also helps to explain why its few cultural references seem a bit out of date: W. H. Auden and Stephen Spender, both of whom the character Christopher quotes, are more closely associated with the 1930s (at the end of which decade, Auden famously emigrated to the USA). A Rodin sculpture and a Picasso etching are mentioned—hardly the cutting edge of new art in contemporary London. This adds to a general impression that, notwithstanding their pretensions to cultural significance, these men are all marginal to London's real literary and artistic scenes. They are just a little bit out of touch.

Popular culture is hardly visible at all. Nicholas does go to the cinema, but we are not told what he sees. Only when his landlady has a few critical words to say about Diana Dors do we get the slightest whiff of what the majority of Londoners would have been consuming in their cultural lives. Only Christopher mentions anything that seems to have got into the book during its revision for publication in the late 1950s. At one point, he says 'I'm not an existentialist.' This is, characteristically, a statement not of philosophical principle but of incapacity—and, moreover, of incapacity for which he disclaims responsibility: 'No one has ever been able to explain it to me as a layman.' But at least he is aware of a trend.

Christopher also says to Michael, who has served in the Royal Air Force, 'Living in the peaceful welfare state is terribly frustrating. You'll just have to join the ranks of the angry young men and suffer.' The birth-date of the British welfare state tends to be given as July 1948, when National Assistance, National Insurance and the National Health Service came into force. The writer Leslie Paul published an autobiography called *Angry Young Man* in 1951. His expression was then taken up to describe the characteristics, or the mood, of a generation. It became a particularly important epithet in reference to characters in contemporary drama. Christopher's remark seems to be guiding Michael towards the genuine crucible of artistic activity in London, a long way further down the social scale than the snobbish Patrick.

Common accounts of the immediate post-war period in Britain offer a diorama of unrelieved gloom: austerity, social conformity, surveillance, puritanism, Cold War paranoia, nuclear anxiety . . . But the characters in the book seem detached from this context: Patrick is rich enough to rise above it, and for as long as he enables them, his protégés follow him into a realm above income, almost above politics. What few political references there are might have been written in the original 1940s version or in the 1950s re-write. Lord Winterborn, whom Patrick regards as a 'mad socialist', is said to be still upset at not having been offered a Cabinet post by the 1945-1951 Labour Government of Clement Attlee. Stuart Andrews wonders if the government (but which government?) is going to call a general election—clearly, the sort of question an editor needs to be asking himself. Patrick thinks Greece an unsuitable place to visit with his new protégé, presumably because of ongoing problems caused by British involvement in Cyprus.

If it is satire, what is it satirising? There is too little identifiable social context for it to be a political commentary. Yet, for those in the know, it must have been a rather obvious *roman à clef*, based on the lives of easily identified, living members of the English literary scene. Michael Nelson had some experience of literary London, having worked as secretary to John Lehmann (1907-1987), a poet and the prominent editor of *New Writing* (later to be reincarnated as *Penguin New Writing*). It is clear that he had met enough of the literati to know how some of them operated, and it seems possible that he had been on the receiving end of enough of their disdain to have wanted to get his own back. How many readers will have been aware of it is open to question, but for certain insiders Ronnie Gras is based on Cyril Connolly (1903-1974), editor of the literary magazine *Horizon*. Patrick is based on Peter Watson (1908-1956), who had co-founded *Horizon* with Connolly, funded it and acted as its art editor. Christopher is based on the poet Stephen Spender (1909-1995), who also worked on the magazine. And Nicholas, fecklessly passive and lacking in initiative, is a rather unattractive (even if physically desirable) authorial self-portrait: a boy seeking an effortless entry to to the world of the arts; or rather, to its upper stratum, where money is no object. (And, as we all know, that is not where any art of real quality is ever created.)

The novel begins in a manner both outspoken and vague: 'He was very, very rich.' This is not exactly Jane Austen, whose opening paragraphs tend to locate her characters financially; but it does what it needs to. It tells us what people know about Patrick, why he is admired, and the source of his power over other men. He is the sort of man who returns to London because it is raining in Paris. He dislikes anything he cannot control. Nicholas is apparently closeted: 'I wish you wouldn't do that in public,' he says when Patrick tries to hand him some money in the bank; 'It makes me feel uncomfortable.' And yet, even while he is saying this, he has taken Patrick by the arm to lead him down the steps of the bank to his car. So it is not the mere fact of an intimate relationship that he is trying to hide, but a monetary arrangement. It is not that he fears being thought homosexual, but that he does not want to look like a kept boy. It is no accident, thinking of the inscription of identities, that the more tense moments in the incipient career of a semi-prostitute take shape around signatures: the counter-signing of a restaurant bill, the failure to sign a cheque . . . Patrick is probably better off with a working-class boy than with the likes of Nicholas. Thinking of himself as a Pygmalion-figure, an artist in the flesh, he needs someone he can manipulate, a male Galatea whose tastes and teeth he can re-shape to meet his own impossible standards.

There is a rather chilling scene in which a valet attached to Patrick's apartment building intimidates Nicholas, clearly aware that he is just another in a line of younger men who have passed through Patrick's flat. Nicholas is so cowed by the insinuations of this man that he imagines he might say, at any moment, 'Come off it. Stop giving yourself airs. I know all about you. You're just another one-night stand. At least my job's steadier than yours.' Even without saying anything so impertinent, the valet exudes an air of menace, perhaps more of a threat to the absent Patrick than to Nicholas, whom he has identified as a mere transient and there-fore of no consequence. Any man so patently in the know about

Patrick's only flimsily discreet personal life is a potential black-mailer. The fact that this is not mentioned shows the extent to which Michael Nelson deliberately steps aside from the expected script about the position of the homosexual in society. Reading this scene in 1958, a homosexual reader would have shuddered of his own accord.

GREGORY WOODS

November 29, 2013

A ROOM IN CHELSEA SQUARE

ONE

HE was very, very rich.

'Ninety, ninety-five, one hundred,' counted the cashier. 'There you are, sir. Beautiful morning for the time of year, isn't it?'

'I suppose it is,' said Patrick. He picked up the pile of five-pound notes. 'Dear me. They won't fit into my note case.'

The cashier was perplexed. 'Can I help you, sir?'

'No, no. There's nothing to be done about it. Whoever designed it must have been crazy. I shall have to buy myself another one, that's all.'

He divided the bundle into halves and slipped them into the pockets of his tweed coat.

So far it had been a good morning. To begin with it was a beautiful day. London was almost bearable; not quite, but London wasn't Paris. Still, it wouldn't be long before he was back in France. It was just a question of laying his hands on enough francs. It was infuriating to be told what he could and what he couldn't do with his money by a crowd of politicians and economists who kept changing their minds. What was the point of money if one wasn't allowed to spend it? Over his breakfast of orange juice and rusks he had flicked over the counterfoils of his cheque book. It had been a delightful surprise to discover that there was more to his credit than there had been at the beginning of the year. It must have come from the rents on the Paddington property which Mummy had left him. He would ask his lawyers about it. It might even be fun to go and see who lived in Paddington. At all events it would pass an hour or two.

Yes, it had been a splendid morning. He had drunk just a little too much the previous night, and before breakfast there had been a nasty moment when it looked as if he was in for a tiresome day. He had been on the point of calling his doctor. In fact, he had stretched out his hand to pick up the telephone, when he had

3

caught sight of a letter lying among the unopened mail on the eiderdown. The writing on the envelope had immediately made him feel very much better. When he had read the letter he had forgotten that he had felt the slightest bit ill.

As he walked down Piccadilly towards Bond Street, he admitted to himself that it wasn't the morning or the thought of returning to his Paris house which was making him feel so young, but the letter from Nicholas Milestone.

How very sensible he had been to motor down to that dreary funeral in Rochester. But one was expected to go to the funerals of old family servants. He had noticed Nicholas the moment they had gone into the church, but it was not until after the service that he'd been able to get into conversation with him. He'd been writing down the names on the cards attached to the quite hideous wreaths in his funny little reporter's notebook. He really was too sweet; young and so much more amusing than all the boring people in London. Good looking too, with his up-turned nose and floppy hair. But above all he was young. Not that he was old himself. Nobody could throw his age in his face. His forty-four, forty-five years, had failed to spoil his face or figure. He still retained that schoolboy charm which he went to such lengths to preserve. It was just a question of taking care of oneself; not too much food or drink and above all the right clothes. In his light well-tailored suits he could easily pass for thirty-five, or even less. So many of his friends didn't pay enough attention to their clothes. They aged themselves needlessly through thoughtless dressing. Clothes were so very good for morale as well. Whenever he felt the slightest bit unhappy about his age, he always went out and bought something new. It had never failed him. No, all considered, he felt and sometimes looked the very same boy who had come down from Oxford.

Oxford. For a moment the recollection of his undergraduate days threw a cloud over the sun. It had all been such fun. He had learnt so little. But he had been so very popular. His parties had easily been the gayest in college. And the final party! How the champagne had flowed! How especially delicious the Fortnum hampers had been! What on earth had induced the Warden to come in just as everything had begun to go so splendidly? He had never cared much for the Warden, but it certainly hadn't been politic to call him an old-fashioned suppressed quean in front of everyone. It was certainly a lucky thing for him that his mother had died the day after he had been sent down. She might have been very difficult about money. There were jealous people who said that the shock had killed her. But he knew perfectly well that she had been broken hearted since Daddy's death. Her health had never been good. In fact, death had been a merciful release. Still, it had been a lucky day for him. Life might have been extremely tiresome if she had had time to alter her will.

Half way along Bond Street Patrick turned into his jeweller's.

It was pleasant to pause for a second inside the door and watch the staff converge upon him. They seemed to like him. There was one member of the staff he rather fancied himself. A junior assistant with blond curly hair. His teeth were bad. They could be easily put right by a clever dentist. That man in Zürich was particularly good.

Patrick waved them all aside and waited for the young assistant to approach.

'Good morning, sir. Wonderful morning, isn't it?'

'Is it? I always feel like buying something when the weather's fine, so I suppose it must be. Have you anything you think might amuse me?'

Yes, his teeth were horrid. But how splendidly they would match his hair if they were straightened and polished.

'We have these diamond cuff links in from Paris. I doubt whether you would care for them, sir, but I think you will be impressed by the stones.'

'No, no. They're not *me* at all,' said Patrick. 'In any case I really haven't the time to look at diamonds which I can't possibly afford. I'm looking for something cheap and simple. Just a small present.'

'Would it be for . . . ?'

'My nephew. Someone about your own age.'

'Quite so, sir. A cigarette lighter or perhaps a case?'

'Have you any *bearable* cases?'

'Naturally, sir. These are silver, of course. Quite charmingly worked, don't you think?'

'Far too vulgar,' said Patrick.

He turned and looked into the window. A tray of sapphires sparkled in the sunlight. How charming it would be if one could light a room in exactly the same colour. It might even be original.

'Have you any gold cases?' he asked.

'If you'll excuse me, sir, I'll go and bring some up for you.'

Patrick watched the young man cross the shop. He walked badly. How depressing to think that the legs beneath the dark striped trousers might be bandy and hairy. If there was one thing he could not stand, it was hairy young men. It was always so difficult to find out. So embarrassing to say to prospective boy friends: 'Tell me, before we go any further. Are you hirsute?'

'Good morning, sir. A wonderful morning!'

It was that frightful manager.

'I hadn't noticed it.'

He disliked his gold teeth. There was quite enough of the stuff in the shop without his having to show you more every time he opened his mouth.

'No?' said the manager. 'Well, perhaps it isn't. But no doubt you've just returned from wintering on the Riviera.'

'I have done no such thing. I never stirred from Paris. The south is bedlam.'

'My wife told me the same thing. She said there simply wasn't room to move this year. I'd hoped to go myself, but business, alas, kept me here.'

It was fantastic. Very soon one would have to winter with one's butcher and baker. There wouldn't be a single place left where one could escape and be alone.

'Can I help you, sir? I expect you'd like to see the exquisite cuff links that have just come in from Paris.'

'On the contrary I think the stones have been most carelessly cut,' said Patrick.

'Ah, yes. If you will excuse me, sir?'

The manager bowed from the waist.

The blond assistant reappeared and placed a tray in front of Patrick, who began to examine the cases one by one.

'Tell me,' he said, 'which would you like?'

'It's difficult to say, sir. The prices vary so much.'

'Of course they do. But imagine you're Croesus this morning and can choose whichever one gives you the most pleasure.'

The assistant looked at the cases and pointed at one, smaller though thicker than the others.

'You like that one?' said Patrick. He almost added: 'Then you must have it,' but checked himself in time. He took the case and turned it over in the palm of his hand. 'I think that will do very nicely indeed.'

'Thank you, sir. Will you take it or shall we send it?'

'I want you to post it for me. Now where have I put the address?'

He took Nicholas's letter out of his pocket: 'Here we are. Nicholas Milestone, c/o *The Weekly Tablet*, Rochester. Be sure to register it. And I hope you'll wrap it up in that charming paper of yours. I think your gothic lettering so attractive.'

'We'll do that, sir. Thank you very much.'

Patrick had reached the door when he remembered that he had not asked the price. He went back to the counter where the young man had begun to replace the cases in the tray.

'I'm rather stupid this morning,' he said. 'How much was it?'

'One hundred and fifty guineas, sir.'

'Dear me. What a lot of money for a spring morning. Do you find the spring makes you crazy too?'

'I couldn't say, sir.'

As he stepped into the street it struck Patrick that it certainly was a lot of money to spend on someone whom he had only met once. He would have to be careful. Under no circumstances was he going to make a fool of himself. On the other hand, Nicholas had seemed such a sad young man. It would do him good to have something really amusing for a change. If Nicholas came to London he would have to see about buying him some new clothes. That pin-striped suit of his had been too ghastly to look at besides being threadbare; it should have been given away long ago.

No. It had been a hundred and fifty guineas well spent. It was a pity he couldn't be present when Nicholas opened the package. Would he be silly and send it back? Perhaps he wouldn't realize it was gold. He had better write and tell him; he could introduce the word casually into a letter. He would write to him after lunch and tell him that he'd sent him a little present. It must be terrible for him having to live alone in a provincial town in what he called *digs*. How much did they cost him? Had he said three or was it four pounds a week including all his meals? He must be starving as well as very unhappy. He'd send him something else to cheer him up.

Patrick, you're going to buy yourself a note case, he told himself. You're beginning to lose control.

Nevertheless, he went into the art gallery. He would have a quick look round. It was unlikely that he'd see anything he liked.

The Picasso etching caught his eye. An early one. Just three young men, probably dancers, changing their clothes. Quite delightful but probably terribly expensive. But as he wandered round the gallery he found that he was unable to raise any enthusiasm for what he saw. Everything seemed so bad and dull after the etching by the door. It was so very charming. Just the thing to brighten a bedroom in a provincial villa.

He went into the office.

'What an extraordinary hotch-potch of an exhibition!' he said. 'Apart from the Picasso which I quite like.'

'I'm afraid it's not cheap. But it's quite charming. Still, I'm sure there must be something else here that interests you. Let me take you round myself.'

They walked round the gallery.

The manager stopped in front of a large canvas. 'Now here is something. It's really one of the best examples of the artist's work that has ever passed through my hands.'

'How much?'

The manager looked at the picture and back again at Patrick. 'Five hundred guineas. That's a special price to you.'

'That's fantastic!' exclaimed Patrick.

'I beg your pardon?'

'My dear man, don't beg my pardon. I paid forty pounds for this picture ten years ago in Paris. I sold it because it bored me. Now you're asking me to buy it back for a crazy figure. I suppose you're asking the Bank of England for the Picasso.'

'The Picasso? It's catalogued at a hundred guineas.'

'I'll give you fifty.'

'I'll sell at a loss.'

'As long as you don't do it too often you'll be all right. I want you to send it for me.'

He wrote Nicholas's address on the back of the catalogue.

The day had grown brighter and the air warmer.

Patrick had enjoyed his shopping expedition. He had no regrets. Why should he have? He could afford to indulge himself occasionally. Besides, if all went according to plan his little gifts would bring him greater joys.

'Patrick! How are you, my dear? I haven't seen you for ages.'

Ronnie Gras was coming out of his wine merchant's.

'Don't be stupid, Ronnie. You were at the party last night. I watched you the whole evening hovering over the caviare like a cross between a kestrel and a greedy little schoolboy.'

'Really, Patrick . . .'

'It was fascinating, my dear. But I do think you ought to give up that disgusting habit of licking your fingers. What on earth has happened to your hair? It's turned yellow like old Chinese straw. Don't tell me. You've been having treatment. My dear Ronnie, a man of your intelligence ought to know better. If your hair wants to fall out, the most expensive treatment in the world won't stop it. You big silly baby. All you need, my dear, is to take some gentle exercise and forget your stomach.'

'If you're going to insult me, Patrick, I've no intention of staying here,' said Ronnie. 'It's a morning in a million. I do think on a day like this you might try to be kind to people.'

'But I am being kind, my dear. Don't be so huffy. Come and have a drink and you'll feel much better.'

'I don't want a drink.'

'Not even a teeny weeny *coupe de champagne*?'

'No thank you. Well, perhaps just one glass. That's if you promise not to insult me. You know it ruins my digestion.'

As they walked together down Bond Street, Patrick wondered how he could ever have imagined himself in love with Ronald Gras. Of course it was a long time ago; five years or even six.

Ronnie had been very different then. Even pleasant to look at. But above all he had been, as he could still be sometimes, an amusing conversationalist in an otherwise dull and dreary country. During their short-lived romance Ronnie had held his first exhibition of paintings which the critics had ignored but which he had known to be good. No. He didn't regret the affair. Together they had given the best parties in London. He had never been bored. Then one day, quite suddenly, life with Ronnie had begun to pall. The stories had been repeated once too often; the same reference had been pulled out of the drawer twice in the same evening. And on top of that had been the question of money. It wasn't that Ronnie had no money. By ordinary standards he was rich. But the pace at which he lived had been too terrifying. So they had parted, he on his part amicably, Ronnie somewhat sourly, distressed to see a fortune slip between his chubby fingers.

They were passing Patrick's jeweller's.

'Patrick, what an exquisite necklace. Do let's go in and have a look at it.'

'Of course you shall if you want to,' said Patrick.

They went into the shop.

'It's like going through the gates of heaven,' said Ronnie.

'Do you feel you've grown platinum wings? They'd have to be terribly strong not to let you down with a bump.'

'Did you leave something behind, sir?' asked the assistant.

'No, no. Mr Gras wants to look at the diamond necklace.'

'You never told me you'd been in here before this morning,' Ronnie said crossly.

'Do you think I should have? Here's your necklace. Do you know something, Ronnie? I think it would look terribly chic round your neck. If it'll go round.'

He took the necklace out of its velvet case and held it under Ronnie's chin.

'I can see this little boy loves butter,' he said.

'Don't be ridiculous,' said Ronnie.

'But you like it? Surely you must like it?'

'It's magnificent.'

'Then you must have it.'

'Really, Patrick. What on earth could I do with a diamond neck-lace?'

'Wear it, my dear. You could make it madly smart for men to wear diamonds. After all, everything you wear is smart, Ronnie. You don't want it? What a pity. Is there anything else you would like? Something simple?'

'What are these things?' asked Ronnie pointing to the tray filled with cigarette cases.

'Cases, my dear. You know little boxes in which you carry round those funny little tubes filled with tobacco.'

The assistant said: 'These are the selection you looked at earlier, sir.'

'They're gold,' said Ronnie.

'But of course. Do you know, Ronnie, I believe all that caviare last night has clotted that brilliant brain of yours. First of all you ask me what they are. Now you fail to recognize your favourite colour.'

Ronnie began to examine the cases one by one. 'They're charm-ing. Do you know, Patrick, I've wanted a gold cigarette case for years.'

'Have you, Ronnie? How extraordinary you are! You turned down the offer of that superb necklace, and now you're pining for something as mundane as a cigarette case.'

'I'm a simple person, Patrick. I believe in simplicity above all. That's what's so admirable about Grecian civilization.'

'My dear, I have the very thing for you. I'm sure they're the height of simplicity even if they're not classical. How absolutely adorable!'

He walked to the next counter on which stood a box of ciga-rette lighters, and picked one up.

'You shall have one of these, Ronnie. Don't you think they're charming? Not the slightest bit vulgar.' He spun the wheel and the lighter burst into flame. 'It works too! Isn't that clever?'

The assistant looked worried. 'Those are only cheap lighters, sir. We give them to our customers when they bring their own in for repair.'

'I wouldn't dream of allowing you to *give* me one,' said Patrick.

'It's such bad luck to give away things that have already been given to you. We don't want to bring Mr Gras bad luck, do we? I shall have to pay for it.'

Patrick handed the assistant a five-pound note.

'Now Ronnie, make up your mind and choose the one you like most. You don't want to? Then you'd better have this one. Now what about that champagne you promised me? Where shall we go? The Rialto?'

Ronnie put the lighter in his pocket.

'You gave him five pounds. What about your change?' he said.

'He shall have it,' said Patrick. 'It's such a wonderful morning and I'm sure he's got a friend he can spend it on. Haven't you, young man? Then buy him a little present. But go somewhere where you get your money's worth.'

The young man smiled. 'Thank you very much indeed, sir.'

'Now come along, Ronnie. We'll get the man on the door to call us a taxi to take us to the Rialto.'

'You have to wait hours for a taxi at this time of the morning. Shall I tell them to ring for a car?'

'Rather extravagant, my dear. Could we just manage to walk it? It would be so good for your waistline.'

'Patrick, I've told you already that I'm not prepared to put up with being insulted this morning. I shall go to my club.'

'Don't be silly, Ronnie. I won't say another word. Tell me. How is your art progressing these days?'

'You know perfectly well I've given up painting.'

'Such a pity. You worked quite hard at the time of our little frolic.'

'I wish you wouldn't talk like that,' said Ronnie. 'You know how much I value that year of my life. I've never been the same since you left me.'

'Don't let's go over all that again. It would choke me,' said Patrick. 'I don't see what you've got to complain about. You're one of the most successful men in London and all the women are mad about you. Leaving me was the wisest thing you've ever done.'

'I left you?'

'But of course.'

'I suppose I did,' said Ronnie.

As they went through the swing doors of the Rialto, he decided it was time he altered his version of the story. No longer would he be the poor abandoned artist. Instead he would be the dedicated genius who had chosen the poverty-stricken life of art, when he had been in danger of being swamped by too much material comfort. In any case, that's exactly what had happened. He had not been left. He had walked out on Patrick.

'Which bar do you like?' asked Patrick.

'We can drink champagne in both. No. Wait a minute. They usually have some palatable *friandises* upstairs. I think we'd better go there.'

'*Friandises*, Ronnie? What sort of *friandises*?'

'They vary. Yesterday there was some very nourishing pâté.'

They ascended the wide staircase and went into the bar.

'Where would you like to sit?' said Patrick. 'In the centre so that everyone can see us?'

'What champagne would you like?' asked Ronnie.

'I'm just a simple girl. I'm sure you know the best one. Personally I always ask the waiter. He should know, shouldn't he?'

'Of course he doesn't. I don't understand that side of you, Patrick. You're in one of your difficult moods. I know perfectly well that you're a fair judge of champagne. Why do you have to pretend that you aren't? What would you say to the Clicquot '29? Perhaps it's getting a little old. The '34 would probably be safer.'

'It's rather expensive, isn't it?' said Patrick. 'I believe the non-vintage champagnes here are drinkable; certainly far cheaper. But order what you think you need. I want you to have just what you want.'

'This is my party,' said Ronnie.

'Nonsense, my dear. You wouldn't accept that silly little necklace from me. The least you can let me do is to buy you a bottle of champagne.'

'I've ordered a magnum.'

'Dear me. A magnum then. Don't you think it's rather a lot for one?'

'There are two of us.'

'I know, my dear. Unfortunately I've only time for one glass. I've got to rush off and have my hair done.'

'Your hair looks perfectly all right to me.'

'How dull witted you are this morning. You must know that it isn't just my hair that has to be looked after. That's the trouble with you, Ronnie. You neglect yourself. Or else you're so vain that you think your face takes care of itself. Believe me, it doesn't. If you took half as much trouble over your face as I do over mine, you'd still be good looking. You were quite presentable when I first knew you.'

'They were happy days,' said Ronnie. 'How I wish they could return. As we grow older we acquire wisdom. But our youth has gone. If we could have the two together how formidable we would be! Oh the misery of age!'

'Surely you're not unhappy, my dear?' said Patrick. 'I know you were miserable when you were a painter. But I thought you felt so much better since you'd abandoned that. I always suspected dress designing was much more your métier. Why, everywhere I go I hear people talking of the Gras look. I thought you found it terribly profitable as well.'

'So it is,' said Ronnie. 'But I'm not happy. The days slip by and I never feel that a single one has been my own. Every design I create soon ceases to be mine. It's quickly vulgarized by my horrible firm. Do you think I like to see my inspirations, created for the few remaining crowned heads of Europe, worn by every shop girl on her Saturday night out? It's ghastly, Patrick. Do you know copies from my spring collection are already being worn by the tarts in Brighton? On top of that I have the sniggers of my friends to put up with. Poor Ronnie Gras! He might have been a great artist, but he's sold his soul to trade for cash. I hate it all. But what can I do? I've got to live.'

'Start on your own, my dear,' said Patrick. 'Build up a great new business like grandfather Gras. He made a lot of money, didn't he? Now what was it in?'

'You know quite well.'

'Of course. So hygienic, my dear. Inspiring too. You ought to follow in his footsteps and make the family name resound more loudly in every suburban closet. It would give you something objective to do. A *Zeitgeist* to living.'

Ronnie leaned forward in his chair.

'Listen, Patrick. And please don't laugh at me. I haven't asked you for anything for a long time, have I?'

'I don't think so.'

'I do want to start on my own. I've an idea that's been going round and round in my head for months.'

'How wonderful! It's what I've always been telling you. Is it a drain-pipe line or something quite new?'

'I shall want backing.'

'Ah! Pennies to throw down fresh drains!'

'It's nothing to do with drains. I want to start a magazine. A new fashion magazine. A rival to *Vogue* and *Harper's*.'

'That's fantastic! It's crazy! You wouldn't stand a chance. You wouldn't sell a thousand copies a week. I don't know very much about these things, but I'm quite sure that competition is already so fierce that you wouldn't interest even the lowest housemaid.'

'I haven't the slightest desire to interest such people. This is to be an exclusive magazine. I don't expect it to have a circulation of more than two thousand at the most. That's about the maximum number of intelligent people in this country today. Until I can get them to support me, I shall need some backing. To begin with at any rate.'

'I'm fascinated. Tell me more. What do you get out of it, Ronnie?'

'I shall be the editor. I want to establish something absolutely fresh. I've always thought that fashion is the truest expression of civilization. It expresses the feeling of an age. If you take the music, art and literature of any period of history, you can deduce the fashion of the time. I want to reunite fashion with its progenitors.'

'It certainly would be amusing to relate modern art to corsets,' said Patrick.

'That's not what I want to do at all.'

'Of course it is. My dear Ronnie, remember that I know you very well. There's an old saying, if you can't create, criticize. Funnily enough I think you'd do it very well.'

'Do you think so, Patrick? That's wonderful. I can see you're enthusiastic already.'

'It would be *new*, wouldn't it? But there are a lot of complications. Where is the money to come from? There'd have to be a staff and an office. There'd be your salary. That would be rather a problem.'

'I'm sure I could find a suitable staff.'

'I meant your salary, my dear.'

'That wouldn't present any difficulty. Naturally I wouldn't like to have to take it from you personally. I'd have to pay myself. After all, I'd have to be in a position to write out business cheques. It would be too embarrassing to take real money from you.'

'I quite understand. I tell you what I could do. I could have it sent round to you in notes by messenger. That should be sufficiently impersonal.'

'It would certainly be civilized.'

'My dear, look who's here!' said Patrick.

They turned in their chairs and saw a tall man loitering by the door. He was standing now on one leg, now on the other, and scratching his neck as he looked apprehensively round the bar.

'God, it's Christopher Lyre!' exclaimed Ronnie.

'Just look at that suit,' said Patrick. 'I must ask him where he buys his clothes. He looks like an overgrown schoolboy.'

Christopher noticed them staring at him and immediately hurried towards them.

'Hullo, Patrick. Hullo, Ronnie,' he said. 'Please forgive me if I'm intruding but may I sit down with you? I'm so tall I hate standing up in these grand places. I feel everyone is looking at me as if I had no right to be here. I know I'm not a very good painter, but it still hurts me just as much to be stared at.'

'Come, come. You're terribly famous,' said Patrick.

'Oh, do you really think so? That's awfully kind of you. When I was a small boy I always wanted to be famous. Now that I am I want to be a small boy again. Stephen Spender in one of his better poems says that changing place isn't changing mind. That's terribly true, you know. We all find that out as we grow older. Don't you agree, Ronnie? I should say your life is a frightfully good example. Don't you sometimes wish you could renounce fame and turn back the clock?'

'He's going to. In a kind of way,' said Patrick.

'I'm so glad. But how?' said Christopher.

'He wants to start a new magazine. A fashion magazine with the emphasis on culture and the arts.'

'How terribly good for him,' said Christopher. 'What are you going to call it, Ronnie?'

'My dear Christopher, we haven't got as far as that,' said Ronnie.

'I think you should call it *Eleven*,' said Christopher. 'My school number was eleven. I had my first sexual experience when I was eleven years old. Some people seem to think that was rather late.'

'I really can't see what that has to do with culture,' said Ronnie.

'I think it was rather young, my dear,' said Patrick.

'That's what the headmaster said. I think he was wrong. But it's an awfully good number, don't you think? It sounds so terribly mystical. Patrick, could I be the art editor? I've always wanted to work for a magazine, and it's really going to be yours, isn't it? I mean, although Ronnie's going to edit it, you're going to finance it.'

Patrick smiled. With a wave of his hand Ronnie indicated to the waiter that the glasses needed refilling.

'Have I said something dreadful?' asked Christopher. 'I'm terribly sorry. I can't help speaking the truth. And I'm feeling rather nervous. I've never been in this bar before.'

'Don't lie,' said Ronnie.

'It's true. Last time I tried to come here they turned me away at the door. That's why I've put on my best suit today. I couldn't face being humiliated by that soldier on the door. It's terribly smart here, isn't it? Do you come here often, Ronnie?'

'He practically lives here,' said Patrick. 'What's brought you here this morning, Christopher?'

'It's rather a funny story. It started in Germany. You know I went over to lecture there for the British Council. Well, I met some Air Force boys. There was one I liked terribly and I started to paint him. Unfortunately I didn't have time to finish it. The Germans took up so much of my time. So I asked him to get in touch with me when he came back to England. Yesterday he rang me up and asked me to meet him here. He's out of the Air Force now. Or rather he's been thrown out. But I won't bore you with him. I'm so excited to hear about this new magazine. You will let me be art editor, won't you, Patrick?'

'You must ask Ronnie.'

'It's kind of you to offer your assistance,' said Ronnie. 'But I don't know yet if there's going to be a magazine. If it does materialize I'll keep you in mind.'

'Thank you so much. Now I must go. There's my friend over there.'

He stood up and caught his knee against the table, spilling the champagne from the glasses.

'I'm terribly sorry. You don't think I've drunk too much, do you?'

'I wonder,' said Patrick as he watched Christopher cross the room and go up to the young man by the door, 'I wonder if my intuition is right?'

'What's that?' said Ronnie.

'Intuition, my dear. I'm afraid I must leave you too, Ronnie. That one glass was almost too much for me.'

'I feel wonderful.'

'So you should, my dear. You've drunk most of the magnum.'

'Is it my fault if I find champagne stimulating?' said Ronnie. 'Will you be coming back?'

'No,' said Patrick. He took a gold pencil from his pocket and signed the bill.

'Will you leave something for the waiter, my dear,' he said. 'I never know how much to give them.'

Ronnie fingered the bill. Signing bills at the Rialto must give Patrick a wonderful sense of power. He knew that they were sent to him on the first of each month. Ronnie looked at the signature, illegible and adolescent. It was a pity that he had allowed all that money to slide from his grasp. Some people told him that he had been a fool, but they didn't know that life with Patrick was perpetual torture. They didn't know that Patrick was a sadist. Not a physical but a mental sadist. Ronnie had his self-respect to consider. It had been quite out of the question to go on living with someone who called his appreciation of the art of living, gluttony; who had even been known to refer to him in public as 'Tubby' or worse still, '*mon petit cochon*'.

Ronnie frowned. He took out his wallet and undertipped the waiter.

*

As Patrick walked across the bar he was more and more convinced that it had been one of his most enjoyable mornings. It had started well and grown better. People had been amusing. They hadn't bored him. Ronnie of course wanted money. Perhaps his spring collection was not proving as profitable as people supposed. On the other hand, there was the possibility that he really did want to stop wasting his talents. It would be fun to own a magazine. And there was Nicholas. A magazine might be very useful. Nicholas had been at the back of his mind from the moment that Ronnie had started to talk about a magazine. It would need a staff. Nicholas could be on it. He would bring him to London and launch him on a career. He would have to move carefully. The young were often ridiculously proud, and had even been known to be scared by money.

As he reached the desk to inquire for mail he met Stuart Andrews.

'Good morning, Stuart. How's your naughty little rag going?' he asked.

'Patrick! Come and have a drink. The *Gladiator's* on the up and up. Yes, sir, the public is loving every inch of it.'

'I'm just going.'

'Nonsense.'

They walked across the foyer and sat down in a corner.

'What'll you have? Whisky?' said Stuart.

'Rather brutal this morning, aren't we?' said Patrick. 'Nasty feeling of American gangster films in the air. I really don't want a drink at all. What are you doing in the Rialto, Stuart? Surely your public wouldn't approve of it. Didn't you run an entrancing feature last week headed: "Rase the Rialto to the ground!" I thought your faith was in the people this year.'

'So it is. You'd better watch your step. I'm gunning for the idle rich again this week. Britain has no room for unearned incomes.'

'Dear me. Are we going to have that boring stuff about the dignity of manual labour all over again? It's so unoriginal, Stuart. I suppose you're going to start calling me a social parasite. Take care you don't flog it for too long, my dear. If you pillory me too much the public might think you're being excessively unkind and come over to my side. You'd be surprised at the British Public's sense of fair play.'

'There's something I want to ask you,' said Stuart.

'Ask me? My dear, I'm flattered. I'm afraid I'm rather a stupid person whom nobody takes any notice of.'

'I don't believe it. I'm a little bit worried. Our circulation is fine. Couldn't be better. But the question is, what's going to happen? Are the Government going to the country or not? If they are, I want to start advocating a general election straight away. If not, I don't want to make a fool of myself.'

'How should I know? Really, Stuart, you know that politics bore me stiff.'

'You happen to know the right people. God knows why. But you do.'

'Do I?'

'Yes. Stop being difficult. Bloody difficult as you always were. Plain obstinate.'

'Oh my dear, don't remind me of those days. Such a long time ago that it makes me feel a hundred to think about it. You were so good looking then, and so very ambitious. Do you remember how you only wanted to become the editor of Auntie *Times*? Well, you've got an editorship. Rather different from what we expected, isn't it? The *Daily Gladiator*! I suppose we must thank God for small mercies. At least there's something classical about the name.'

'Dry up,' said Stuart. 'It's easy enough to sneer when you've got more money than you can spend. I wanted money and power. I've earned both. I haven't forgotten what you did for me. I'm grateful.

But climb off your high horse for a minute. I want you to find this out for me.'

'I'll try. Anything to help you, Stuart. It's fascinating to watch you heave yourself up the ladder of success. Mind you don't strain yourself and topple off. In return, there's something I'd like you to do for me.'

'Anything I can.'

'I have a friend on a local newspaper. I want you to offer him a job on the *Gladiator*.'

'O.K. It's a deal. He starts work tomorrow.'

'No, no. I want it done quietly. How shall I say? Warily.'

Stuart began to laugh.

'I don't like the sound of that,' said Patrick. 'It's got a dirty ring about it. I don't want you to pay him too much. It might go to his head, and I should hate to corrupt him. Anyway, he won't be working for you for long.'

'Why?'

'I'm thinking of going into the paper business myself and I shall need staff. It's been such a dull year I feel I want something new to cheer me up.'

'And this little number of yours walks straight into the editorial bed,' said Stuart.

'You always were beautifully tactful. I do think that when you emerge from your chromium-plated palace of lies, you should leave your gladiatorial manners behind.'

'Don't get sore. What's the boy's name?'

Patrick wrote Nicholas's name and address on a piece of paper and gave it to Stuart.

'Such fun to bribe the Press, isn't it?' he said. 'The only trouble is that you're almost too rich now, Stuart. If you're leaving, you could drop me off.'

Christopher crossed the bar conscious that Patrick and Ronnie were watching him.

'Hullo, Mike,' he said. 'How are you? It's nice to see you again after so long.'

'Shall we sit? That's if we can find a seat,' said Michael.

'Let's go somewhere else,' said Christopher. 'I'm not at all happy here. I feel as if I'm being eaten alive. That's terribly painful, you know.'

'As you like,' said Michael. 'Where do you suggest?'

'What about a pub? Pubs are so much more honest than these places. I find pubs make me work. When I come to places like this I'm incapable of doing any work for days afterwards. You see, humanity is ugly at the best of times. But it's ugliest when it tries to be beautiful, because it's being dishonest. Everyone in here is dishonest. They upset me terribly.'

'You always make everything sound difficult,' said Michael.

'I'm terribly sorry. That's what Ronnie is always telling me. Ronnie Gras I mean. You don't know him. He says I stir up clear waters to make them muddy and seem deeper than they really are. That's Nietzsche actually. Not Ronnie Gras. He's terribly good. Nietzsche I mean. When I'm painting I sometimes try and believe I'm a superman.'

'Have you painted much recently?'

'Much too much. None of it is any good, I'm afraid. I'm like a hen that lays unfertilized eggs. It's not a terribly good analogy. What I'm trying to say is that my pictures lack life; they're the product of immense effort but they're all stillborn. I sometimes think that if an artist is going to produce something really alive, he must be loved by someone. That's why good artists are often so promiscuous. Which makes it difficult for them to live in society, because society thinks them immoral. They're not helped by the thousands of bad artists who think that immorality makes them good artists. Anyway, that's why I never come to places like the Rialto. I feel I'm not wanted.'

'I'm sorry I suggested it. Shall we take a taxi?'

'No. Let's walk. It's such a beautiful day. Please don't think it mattered at all that you suggested meeting at the Rialto. I'm sure that while one is young these places seem attractive. But when I was young I was very poor and could only flatten my nose against their panes. Now I've grown up I still feel they're trying to keep me out. I expect you've always been able to go wherever you wanted. That's a terrific advantage.'

'It's not true. I started to go to the so-called smart places when I got my commission. I had enough money for the first time, and my uniform was a pass.'

'What are you doing now?'

'Nothing.'

'Is that a good thing?'

'I wouldn't know. I can't do anything until I know what I want to do, can I?'

'Why did you leave the Air Force?'

'We had an argument. I flew my plane under a bridge. After that they didn't seem to want me any longer. The funny thing is that when I was doing it, I knew they would chuck me out.'

'It was a subconscious protest I expect,' said Christopher. 'You made a mistake in imagining you could be happy in the Air Force, so you got yourself out of it. You couldn't help yourself.'

'That's all very well. But what do I do now? I can't make up my mind what I want to do. Have you any suggestions?'

'I'm afraid not. I'm afraid you're suffering from guilt at having missed the war. You see war, whatever else it may do, makes us forget ourselves. It gives a purpose to our lives. It's a wicked thing to say, but true. Living in the peaceful welfare state is terribly frustrating. We're not equipped to deal with it. We grow bored. You'll just have to join the ranks of the angry young men and suffer.'

'How did you get over it?'

'My case is really rather funny. You see, all generations have to suffer in their own peculiar way. In some ways I think we had a worse time than you. You see, I knew there was going to be a war ten years before the last one was declared, so that when it finally broke out it didn't stimulate me at all. I had already fought my personal battle in Spain. It was then that I realized that history is a force we can't control, and that all we can hope to be is merely a part of it.'

'I haven't the faintest idea what you're talking about. At least you felt like painting. I've seen reproductions of pictures you painted in the 'thirties. Frankly, I think they're the best thing you've done.'

'I'm so glad,' said Christopher. 'Some people were terribly unkind to me about Spain because I insisted that I was an artist and not a soldier. When I went to Madrid I knew that my mission was to paint, not to fight. But the fighting was very close. In fact it was *inside* me, so that I experienced the same sensations as if I was fighting physically. So you see what I mean when I say that my generation has probably suffered more than yours. But it doesn't help me to give you any good advice. But I do know one thing. If you're thinking of taking up painting, the sooner you start the better it'll be for you.'

'That's one thing I don't want to do,' said Michael.

'I'm not being very helpful, am I? I hope you don't mind my trying to help you. People should try and help each other. I remember Wystan Auden once saying to me: "We must love one another or die!" I think it's the best thing he ever said. After that he went to pieces, although I'm still very fond of him. I don't want you to think that I'm criticizing him. It's difficult to talk about him as he works in such a different medium. But creators have something in common after all.'

'What?'

'The act of creation.'

'Where are we going?' asked Michael. 'To a pub, or do we keep walking?'

'Pub? I'm afraid I forgot. How stupid of me. I thought we were going to my studio. Would you like to do that? I feel I could get on with your portrait this afternoon, if you wouldn't mind sitting. But I expect you're dying for a drink. Shall we try this one? I don't know what it's like. But all pubs are pubs, aren't they?'

They sat down at a table in the corner of the saloon bar.

'Talking about wanting to help people, I'd really very much like to help you if I can,' said Christopher.

'Thanks.'

Michael put his hand to his forehead and pushed his hair back from his eyes.

'You're terribly handsome, Mike,' said Christopher. 'You're one of the most beautiful people I've ever seen. I'm sure this portrait is going to mean something. Perhaps the end of my sterile period.'

'I didn't think much of it last time I saw it. I felt that you were going to forget to put me into the triangle at all. I suppose it's fashionable but it's not going to look anything like me. It would be terribly funny to see it in a gallery and make rude remarks about it, only to discover later that it was myself.'

'You're talking like a philistine. I promise you you'll like it when it's finished. Beauty is elusive. I'm going to put it into this picture the moment I trap it. I'm not going to allow it to slip from my grasp.'

'You can't isolate beauty like that,' said Michael. 'In your case I should have said that it was entirely dependent on your vision. It's the essence that exists between your eyes and what you see, or what you think you see.'

'You're terribly clever,' said Christopher. 'I want you to tell me more about this essence.'

'Do you find me funny?'

'No, no. Far from it. I tell you what we'll do. We'll make a mutual assistance pact. While you're wandering and wondering what to do, you must stay with me. I'm afraid my place isn't very grand, but at least it won't cost you anything. In exchange you must tell me more about these beautiful essences.'

'I'd be glad of a bed. I'd like to nurse my modest resources until I've got a job, and rooms cost a fortune. But we'll forget the other nonsense. It's bloody silly imagining that I could teach you a thing. Everyone says you're the best contemporary painter in the country.'

'I know. But one must always try to learn more. That's why Jesus was so wise and good. He believed in teaching. He gathered simple people round him and started to teach them everything he knew. He realized that he was working on fertile soil. Simplicity is the most fertile soil of all. And it's always beautiful. That's why my work has been so influenced by the Minoans and Dorians.'

'Shall we go to your studio?' said Michael.

Stuart Andrews eased himself out of the Rolls. The commissionaire at the door saluted him. Stuart eyed his smart soldierly uniform with approval. He looked up at the neon signs on the face of the building. The lettering was forty feet high. They could easily take another ten feet, he thought. What the hell did that architect think he was about with all his highfalutin talk of per-spective? In any case he wasn't interested in perspective. It gave him enormous pleasure to leave the building at night and see the evidence of his success against the London sky. The bigger the let-tering, the greater his success.

Today the chromium-fronted building gleamed in the sunshine. He knew that his Fleet Street enemies called it the Silver Coffin. Let them. It made no difference to the circulation of the *Gladiator*, which soared weekly. He knew what the British public wanted. It wanted what he made it want. Two things only. Sex and scapegoats. He never forgot these two words. They paid handsome dividends.

'Beautiful day, sir,' said the commissionaire.

'Sure, Charles. Swell day. Have a sandwich sent up to my office right away. Make sure it's fresh.'

That was another factor which had contributed to his success. Simplicity. Down-to-earthness. He was as happy with a sandwich as he was dining at the smartest restaurant in London. Social life was unprofitable. It burnt up energy and gave no return. He could go where he liked. Every door was open to him. But he was first and foremost a newspaper man. His place was at his desk on the third floor of the *Gladiator*. He'd rather eat a snack there than waste time at the Rialto with a crowd of idlers who imagined themselves smart.

He went into his office, switched on the intercommunication set and asked the assistant editor to join him.

'How's she going, Tom?'

'Fine, sir. We've bannered the fire story. Should have the whole fire service on their toes holding their backsides.'

'How did the fire start?'

'No idea. They couldn't bring it under control because the hoses wouldn't reach. So I thought we'd play the child angle and ginger them up a bit.'

'What's the banner?'

'Do you want your baby burnt alive?'

'Fine. Got a good picture?'

'The news editor's youngest. Sweet looking kid. It should send them all right.'

'Blow it up big. Now I want one of the boys to do a job for me. Who's been working extra hard and could do with a few hours off?'

'John Berlin. He's been putting in a lot of hours on prostitution in London parks.'

'He'll do. I'm taking on a new man. I'll let you know what you're to put him on later. Send Berlin in right away.'

Three minutes later Berlin knocked at the door and came into the office.

'Take a pew, John. That stuff you've been turning out is swell. Good and hot. Been working hard at it?'

'Fairly, sir.'

'Only fairly?'

'You see, sir, my kid's been teething and kicking up such a hell of a shindy that I haven't been able to get down to work until late.'

'Did you take a look round the parks?'

'No, sir. I find my imagination produces the best results.'

'That's the idea. I've a job for you. It's confidential, by the way. Take a car down to Rochester this afternoon. I want you to contact a kid on the local for me. Here's his address. His name's Nicholas Milestone.'

TWO

'Now I ask you, Mr Milestone. Is that what you call art?' exclaimed Nicholas's landlady as she stood with her hands on her hips looking at the Picasso etching with unconcealed disapproval. 'Give me the marmalade cat in the parlour any day. Why, it's not even decent. What do the three of them think they're doing gallivanting around like that without a stitch of clothing on? Mark my words, that's the kind of thing that causes revolutions. It's the same at the pictures. Diana Dors indeed! Give me the old-timers, I say.'

Nicholas let the Picasso hang for twenty-four hours against the mauve-flowered paper. Then he could stand it no longer. They didn't hit it off together. He took it down and put it in the trunk under his bed.

When he went to his room the following evening the marmalade cat had taken its place. An out-of-date calendar hung from the bottom of the frame to which it was attached by a strip of pale blue ribbon.

The cat certainly looked more at home than the three young men against the mauve herbaceous border.

'My God! What a sparkler! Where did you pick that up, son?' said the assistant editor of the Rochester *Weekly Tablet*. 'That wasn't first prize for the largest marrow at the Four Square Gospellers' flower show.'

Nicholas replaced the case in his pocket, and lit his cigarette. 'It came by post this morning.'

'From your fairy godmother, eh?'

'That's it.'

The assistant editor leant back in his chair and laughed. 'What the devil are you going to put in it? You'll have to give up those cheap fags you usually buy. So you're really going to leave us. Where did you say you're off to?'

'You know quite well. The *Gladiator*.'

'Jesus!'

'What's the matter with it?'

'What's right with it, you mean. How did you fiddle it?'

'Through John Berlin. The fellow who came down here on that dead-end Teddy-boy story.'

'He offered you the job, did he? Well, well, everything's certainly come your way. Gold case. Job on a national. Fleet Street seems paved with gold for little boys these days. Sure you know what you're about? Do you think you'll stand the racket?'

'Should I have turned it down?'

'I don't know. Whatever I said you'd have done the opposite, because you'd have told yourself that it was just an old provincial hack talking. But if it doesn't turn out quite as you dreamt, don't think you've been badly treated.'

'It's a chance in a million.'

'Of course it is, my boy. Jolly good luck to you. Keep your nose to the grindstone, and one day, provided you've worked hard enough, you may be a newspaper man.'

Nicholas found an empty carriage, kicked off his shoes, and put his feet up on the opposite seat. Soon he would be travelling across Europe by continental express. He would be on a flying visit to Tibet to sum up the political situation. Now he was being granted an exclusive interview by the President of the United States. He was at Sandringham for the week-end. He had shot well and had his share of the bag. Her Majesty leant across the table and wagged a royal finger at him. 'You know more than I do, Mr Milestone.' He smiled discreetly. 'That's my job, ma'am.' Back in London a harassed Prime Minister growled in his ear. 'Thank God I took your advice, Nicholas.'

A porter opened the door of the carriage and lifted the suitcase off the rack. Nicholas stepped off the train and looked along the platform. There was no sign of Patrick. He must have changed his mind and decided not to come and meet him. Nicholas followed the porter and gave up his ticket at the barrier.

'Nicky! Nicky!'

He turned and saw a gloved hand waving at him from the window of a taxi.

'My dear, how are you?' said Patrick. 'I'm so sorry not to have met you on the platform. But I just can't face the dirt. It's quite the filthiest station in London. Jump in. Here you are, porter.' He tipped the porter before Nicholas had time to feel in his own pocket.

'It's jolly kind of you to meet me, Patrick,' said Nicholas. 'I really didn't expect you. You always seem to have so much to do.'

'Never too busy to welcome a new friend. Especially on such an important occasion. The great journalist on the threshold of his career! It's so exciting. Where would you like to go?'

'I'd better drop my things first.'

'Don't be silly. They can wait. Anyway, you've got nothing with you except one baby case. We'll lunch first. We can take it round afterwards. Where are you going to live? I don't think you told me in your letter.'

'A friend of mine has found me a room in Chelsea Square.'

'How fashionable. Just the place for the ace boy of the *Gladiator*.'

'I didn't know it was fashionable.'

Patrick patted Nicholas on the arm. 'If it wasn't before, now that you've decided to live there, it very soon will be. Now don't frown. I always chatter away like this when I'm happy, my dear. Where do you think we ought to lunch? I suppose it depends where we are.'

'Regent's Park.'

'So we are. How fantastic! For one moment I thought we were in Paris. You must call on me there just as soon as your paper sends you flying round the world. I'm afraid my house may not be grand enough for you by then. But it's comfortable. . . . Be an angel and tell the driver to take us to the Rialto. I hope you won't mind eating there.'

When they got out of the taxi Patrick said: 'Ask the man with all those medals for some money will you, my dear?'

'Money?'

'For the taxi man. I always drop everything if I try to pay them myself.'

'What shall I do with my things?' said Nicholas.

'*Things?* Oh, I see, your sad and solitary suitcase. I should ask Mr Medals, if I were you. I'm sure if you're nice to him, he'll take good care of it.'

They walked through the revolving doors into the foyer.

'Now my dear, we must have a drink. I'm sure you're absolutely exhausted after all that nonsense. You go on into the bar. I've got to make a telephone call. I'll join you in two minutes. Don't wait for me. Order what you feel like.'

'Which bar?'

'It's more amusing upstairs.'

He left Nicholas and walked across the foyer. On the way he noticed a lift boy whom he had not seen before. He walked towards the lift humming quietly to himself. 'No customers? Perhaps you'd take me right to the top.'

The lift ascended and stopped on the top floor.

Patrick looked at the lift boy. 'Thank you so much. Now perhaps you'd take me down again. I know it's strange, but I love riding up and down in lifts. I expect you do too.'

He left the lift and walked to the reception desk.

'I wonder if you can help me,' he said. 'I want one of those expensive rooms of yours that overlook the park.'

'I very much regret that none of them is free at the moment, sir. What was it exactly that you were wanting?'

'Two single rooms.'

'I'm afraid that all we can offer you is the suite you occupied on your last visit, sir.'

'Why didn't you say so to begin with? Have my luggage taken up.'

'How long will you be staying, sir?'

'My dear man, how can I say? Time is so tiresome, don't you think?'

He went slowly up the stairs into the bar. There was no hurry for Nicholas to rush off to some squalid little room in Chelsea. He must have a holiday first. In any case he owed Nicholas a celebration. He would have to take care not to frighten him. At the moment it was painfully obvious that all Nicholas wanted to do was to start work on Stuart's ghastly rag. Monday would be quite soon enough for him to start thinking about that. Tomorrow they might lunch at the Connaught. Afterwards they could go to a concert, or if it was fine, drive down to the country for the afternoon.

'What would you like to drink, Patrick?' said Nicholas.

'Don't be silly, my dear. This is my treat and I don't want any more nonsense.'

'I'd like to buy you a drink.'

'How sweet. Just this once only. An iced tomato juice.'

'Are you sure?'

'Quite, my dear. It's so kind to the figure. Dear me, that reminds me. I should have telephoned Ronnie this morning. Never mind. He's sure to come here. Do look out for him, won't you?'

'Ronnie?'

'How silly of me. You don't know him, of course. Ronnie Gras. You must meet him. He's quite fantastic and ever so greedy. But I adore him. He's one of the few amusing people left in England. He knows it too.'

'How shall I recognize him?'

'Look for something large, my dear.' He waved towards a man who had just come into the bar.

'Is that him?'

'No, no, my dear. That's Lord Winterborn. Such a bore! Lives in a fantastic gothic château in Surrey surrounded by jade and parrots. Made a fortune in the war out of shells or fuses or something dangerous, the wicked old thing. He's a mad socialist. They say he was terribly upset when the Labour Government didn't offer him a post in the Cabinet. They were absolutely right of course. The popular Press wouldn't have stood for it.'

'Do you know anything about the *Gladiator*?' asked Nicholas. 'I believe it's terribly tough.'

'Not tough, my dear; just rather damp and nasty. Let me think. Whom do I know there? I've met Stuart Andrews. He's the editor. He thinks he's terribly tough, but *au fond* he's as tame as a bear in the zoo.'

'I hope I'm not being an awful bore talking about my job,' said Nicholas. 'I can't help asking myself what it's going to be like. I was so very lucky to get it. Now I'm nervous because I'm not at all sure what I've let myself in for. I'm frightened I haven't had enough experience.'

'Don't be silly, my dear,' said Patrick. 'If you write for the *Gladiator* as well as you write letters, you'll soon have the public at your feet. . . . That tomato juice was quite delicious. . . . What would you say to a sip of champagne before we lunch? You're quite happy to eat here, are you?'

'I should love it. I've never been here before.'

'How charming! What fun for our rustic writer! We'll eat here every day until you get tired of it. We'll go and call on the chef and ask him to cook us something delicious. It's years since I've done that. Now what kind of champagne would you like? Sweet or dry?'

'I don't mind.'

'Then let's have something half and half. I knew it! There's Ronnie!'

Ronnie walked across the bar to the table where they were sitting.

'Ronnie, you're just in time,' said Patrick. 'This is Nicholas Milestone.'

Nicholas stood up and said: 'How do you do, sir?'

'Oh, do sit down, please,' said Ronnie.

'You mustn't call people sir, Nicky,' said Patrick. 'It makes them feel so terribly old.'

Ronnie was looking at the bottle of champagne which the waiter had placed on the table.

'I know you're going to complain because I've ordered medium champagne,' said Patrick. 'It was very naughty of me knowing that you'd be coming to join us. You don't know Ronnie, Nicholas, but he has a most canny nose. He can sniff out a bottle of champagne like one of those clever animals that can smell water hundreds of miles away.'

Nicholas flushed with embarrassment.

'I'm only joking, Ronnie,' said Patrick. He patted Ronnie on the knee. 'You've got a very pretty nose. I like it. Don't you, Nicky?'

'Have you seen that madman Christopher?' asked Ronnie.

'Not today,' said Patrick.

'I don't know what he thinks he's up to. He's rushing around the place telling everyone that he's going to be the art editor of my new magazine. It's much too premature. What's more, I'm not at all sure that I want my name coupled with his. You've got to put a stop to it at once, Patrick.'

'What can I do?' said Patrick. 'I know it's rather naughty of him. But on the other hand it's quite good publicity. I should say the more people who start talking about *Eleven*, the greater support it'll receive when it finally does appear.'

'So you've made up your mind!' said Ronnie excitedly. 'You're willing to let me try?'

'I think it would be rather amusing. I was going to telephone you this morning to tell you so, but I had to rush out and it went right out of my mind.'

'You might have spared me a minute,' said Ronnie. 'You must have known how much it was worrying me. My *Angst* has been absolutely dreadful this last week.'

'It was rather wicked of me,' said Patrick.

'We can't call it *Eleven*,' said Ronnie.

'I think it's rather a good name. So does your art editor.'

'He's an irresponsible lunatic.'

'You mustn't call your associate a lunatic.'

'But he's not my art editor,' said Ronnie.

'Oh dear! When he telephoned me yesterday I told him that he could be. He was madly enthusiastic. We can't disappoint him now, can we?'

'But, Patrick, you must see that if I'm going to be the editor, I must be allowed to choose my own staff.'

'So you shall. I *am* sorry about Christopher, but I don't see how I can go back on my word.'

'I suppose he'll have to stay. Now I was thinking that . . .'

'We're boring Nicky,' said Patrick.

'Of course you're not,' said Nicholas.

'But we are. What's more it's time for lunch. If you'll telephone me about tea time, Ronnie, we'll continue this business man's conversation.'

'We must all get together and go into it thoroughly,' said Ronnie.

'We'll do that. . . . Do finish the champagne if you can bear it.'

Nicholas got up from his chair and held out his hand. Ronnie ignored it. He was fully occupied filling his glass. There was a gleam in his eye which reminded Nicholas of a chimpanzee gazing at a bunch of bananas.

'Come on, Nicky. He's counting the bubbles,' said Patrick.

As they walked out of the bar Nicholas said: 'What an extraordinary looking man. He looks just like a chimpanzee.'

Patrick burst out laughing. 'Ronnie the Chimp! How right you are. Remind me to tell him. He'll be so upset when he hears what the younger generation call him.'

Nicholas couldn't understand why Patrick was so amused by his very obvious remark. Anyone could see the resemblance. He had only made it because he had been irritated by Ronnie's cool attitude towards him.

'What did you say Ronnie's other name is?' he asked.

'The Chimp's? Gras. Didn't you recognize that famous face? I'm afraid he's not going to like you very much, my dear.'

'You don't seem very fond of him.'

'He's one of my oldest friends. I only tease him because he's so fantastically conceited.'

'He should make a good editor then.'

'I wonder.'

'If you're so dubious I don't see why you're going to start this magazine.'

'How *naif* you are. Can't you see what fun it will be? I've never attempted anything quite so constructive before. But don't let's have any more of this boring business talk. We've so much to do, and after lunch I've got to call in at the gallery. I'm told Christopher's new pictures are incredible.'

'I ought to move into my room first,' said Nicholas.

'So you shall. But there's no mad hurry. We can easily arrange for your luggage to be sent round from here. Tell me, what have you got in that funny little suitcase? You're so worried about it, I do believe it must be gold.'

'Only a few clothes. My other stuff is coming up later.'

'I hope you see it, my dear. Everything is stolen these days. I had two crates of special oranges sent all the way from Tangiers to my favourite aunt. Would you believe it? After coming all that way they disappeared between Southampton and Waterloo.'

'I never thought of you as having a family,' said Nicholas.

'I'll tell you about them one day,' said Patrick. 'Oh dear, the thought of them has flattened the soufflé. . . . I've been talking so much I've forgotten to ask you what you'd like to drink? A delicious bottle of wine?'

'If you're going to have some.'

'Vichy water for me.'

'Then I'll have the same.'

'Two little collaborators together! Would you have collaborated if the Germans had come here, Nicky?'

'I'd have been too young to know much about it,' said Nicholas. 'If I'd been old enough, I like to think not. It's so easy to criticize. One doesn't know how one would react to pressure until it has actually been applied. What would you have done, Patrick?'

'I should have made for America. It's really the only safe place to live these days. I suppose that's why they make it so terribly difficult for us to go there. Would you like to go to America, Nicky?'

'Very much.'

'Then we must see what we can do to get you there. I'm sure your paper needs a good correspondent in New York. They'll have to send you. Then I'll fly over and you can come and interview me when I step off the plane.'

'You're looking a long way ahead.'

Patrick put his napkin on the table and gazed through the windows that overlooked the park. 'My dear, look at those people out there eating from newspapers. Horrible, aren't they? Why must they be so drab and dreary? I suppose it's because they've no ambition; they don't want to change. If you want anything hard enough, you can always get it. Take it from me, my dear. You're young and rather nice. Believe me, there's nothing you can't have if you want it and are determined to have it. I'm not saying that you'll get it for nothing. You'll have to pay a nominal price for it.'

'You're talking in riddles,' said Nicholas.

'So I am. I think we'd better have coffee outside. I can't bear to sit here another minute watching those frightful people.'

When they went into the foyer he said: 'Sit down there, while I order the coffee.'

'It's rather central.'

'I want everybody to see you.'

As he lit a cigarette Nicholas felt that the day was gradually slipping out of his control. He had made a mistake in letting Patrick know the time of his arrival. He should have come quietly to London, moved into his room, and prepared himself for work the following Monday. It would have been far more sensible to have got in touch with Patrick when he had settled down and established himself.

He looked up at the clock. It was already three. He couldn't think of a likely sounding excuse. He would have to go with Patrick to the gallery.

He dropped a lump of sugar into his coffee and watched the bubbles rise to the surface. It was no good pretending that he didn't know why Patrick was taking such an interest in him. So far it all seemed harmless enough. Still, he would have liked to know more about Patrick.

'Day dreaming? How serious you look! A pound for your thoughts!' said Patrick.

'Nothing.'

'That's what all little boys say. Are they worth more than a pound?'

He took out a five-pound note and rolled it into a spill. He leant towards Nicholas and tickled him with it behind the ear.

'Ah, the little boy likes cream. Five lovely pounds for your thoughts, my dear.'

Nicholas pushed the note to one side.

'Everyone's looking at us,' he said.

'Not at us. At you, my dear,' said Patrick.

He started to tickle Nicholas on the back of the neck with the note.

'Please, Patrick. I hate being tickled.'

Patrick stroked his own cheek with the note.

'Does it tickle? So it does. You'd better tell me the truth or I shall tickle you again.'

'I was thinking how suddenly my life had changed,' said Nicholas. 'A week ago I wouldn't have believed you if you'd told me I'd be sitting here today.'

'How amusing,' said Patrick. 'There!' He tucked the note in the pocket of Nicholas's coat. 'So much prettier than a flower! Yes, very *chic*, my dear.'

Nicholas took the note and handed it back to Patrick who shook his head and laughed. Nicholas hurriedly stuffed the note into his trouser pocket.

As they came out of the Rialto into the street, Nicholas noticed a Rolls drawn into the kerb.

'What a grand car,' said Patrick. 'Do you think it's big enough for us, Nicky? Or shall I send it back and tell them to send something larger?'

The chauffeur held open the door.

'Oh look, there's a microphone,' said Patrick as he sat down. 'Will you navigate, Nicky? I'd love to drive round and round with you as my navigator. Let's order it for Monday and spend the whole day shopping.'

'I'll be working on Monday,' said Nicholas.

'So you will be. But it would be fun, don't you think? There's plenty of room for parcels in here. Why don't we do a little shopping now? I'm sure you ought to have something new to wear on Monday; a pork-pie hat and a camel-hair coat.'

'I never wear a hat.'

'You'll have to if you're going to be a star reporter.'

'It's getting late. I think we ought to go straight to the gallery,' said Nicholas.

'You enjoy looking at pictures?'

'I think so. If I like them.'

'I never know what I like. I'm always buying pictures which I'm sure I'm going to be able to go on looking at for ever. Then one sad morning I wake up to find they bore me. I don't expect we'll find anything this afternoon. Which is rather a pity. I do so desperately need something for the bathroom.'

'The bathroom?'

'Quite the best place for looking at pictures. Up to a few days ago I had a charming Manet in mine. Then I realized that it disapproved of me in the bath, so out it had to go.'

'Nicky! I never expected to meet you here!'

'You've friends everywhere,' said Patrick.

'Michael, how are you? What are you doing? I'm just about to go round to Chelsea Square. Thanks a lot for finding me a room. You don't know Patrick, do you?'

'I've heard a lot about you,' said Michael.

'But nobody knows me,' said Patrick.

'You're starting a new magazine, aren't you? Christopher can't stop talking about it.'

'Dear Christopher. He's such an enthusiast,' said Patrick. 'Is he here?'

'Over in the far corner. He's rather upset because they've hung two of his pictures upside down,' said Michael.

'I must go and congratulate him,' said Patrick.

Michael said: 'Well, Nick, how did you get hold of that one? Christopher says he's one of the richest men in England.'

'Is he?'

'Christopher can't stop talking about him.'

'How do you know Christopher?'

'He's finishing a portrait of me. One he started when I was still a boy in blue. But never mind him. What was all the rush about my finding a room for you?'

'I'm starting work on the *Gladiator*.'

'Good for you. My God! Aren't these pictures sods? Come and meet Chris. He'll tell us all about them.'

They walked across the gallery and joined Christopher who was talking earnestly to Patrick.

'Chris, this is an old friend of mine, Nicholas Milestone,' said Michael.

'Patrick has just been telling me all about you, Nicholas. I'm so glad Mike was here with me. It's so terribly exciting to run into old friends unexpectedly.'

'Do you think any of Christopher's pictures would look well in the bathroom?' asked Patrick.

'In the bath. With the taps on,' said Michael.

'Oh, you are unkind, Mike,' cried Christopher. 'He's always teasing me about my work, Nicholas. He pretends he's a philistine. But he's got a far better critical sense than I have. I suppose it's good for me to be hurt. It spurs me on to do better work. I doubt whether an artist can ever achieve his object. But it's important that he should believe he can. Otherwise he would give up and turn his face to the wall!'

'From boredom?' said Michael.

'How naughty you are,' said Patrick. 'But I sympathize. Boredom terrifies me more than anything else. Now take me round, Christopher. You can tell me which are good. If you see anything you like, Nicky, make a note of it. Something suitable for the bathroom.'

Christopher took Patrick by the arm and led him away.

'I don't know what to make of Patrick,' said Nicholas.

'Don't be so bloody ingenuous,' said Michael. 'Let's go and choose a pretty picture. We can plan what to do this evening at the same time.'

'I must move into my room sometime,' said Nicholas.

'That can wait.'

'That's what everybody keeps telling me.'

'We'll get Christopher to take us out to dinner,' said Michael. 'He's sold a lot of pictures so he should have stacks of cash. If he won't play, we can try your boy friend.'

'He's not my boy friend.'

'Don't be so bloody brittle. You don't have to pretend with me. As if I'd care. What about this one for the bathroom?'

Patrick and Christopher rejoined them as they stood facing a large canvas.

'Fascinating,' said Patrick. He stepped forward and examined the picture closely. 'You seem to have squeezed the paint on straight from the tube. It *is* clever. But could I look at it through *steam*? You'll have to decide for me, Nicky. Yes or no?'

The three of them waited for Nicholas to answer. He looked at the picture and back at them.

'If you like it, Patrick . . .' he began.

'It's what *you* like,' said Patrick. 'You must be a baby Solomon.'

'You'll have to cut it in half to get it into the bathroom anyway,' said Michael.

'If it's terribly expensive . . .' said Nicholas.

'I'm sure it is,' said Patrick.

'I shouldn't buy it,' said Nicholas.

'Don't let stupid pennies influence your judgment,' said Patrick. 'Do you like it? That's what you must decide. I just can't make up my mind.'

'I don't like it.'

'Then there's no point in having it, is there?' said Patrick. He looked at his watch. 'After hearing such a popular verdict, I suggest it's time we all had tea.'

'What fun!' said Christopher. 'I can't remember when I last had tea. You did mean all four of us, didn't you, Patrick? Where shall we go? Somewhere terribly smart like the Ritz?'

'I think we'll go to my flat. It'll be so much less crowded there.'

Christopher whispered to Michael: 'We are in luck. His flat's full of the most wonderful things. He only invites his closest friends. Not very often at that.'

Patrick, who had already got into the car, called out: 'Stop whispering like a furtive schoolboy, Christopher, and get in. You're behaving exactly as if it were the end of term.'

'I'm so excited about the magazine that I can't help it,' said Christopher. 'I lay awake all last night thinking about the cover of the first number. I couldn't make up my mind whether to use letters or figures. On the whole I'm in favour of figures. Which would you prefer?'

'It's nothing to do with me,' said Patrick. 'You'll have to discuss it with Ronnie. You'll find he's bubbling with ideas. He telephones me every morning about it.'

'That's why I can never get through to you,' said Christopher. 'It makes me rather jealous. I'd love my telephone to keep ringing all morning. It would make me feel so important.'

'You'd soon start leaving the receiver off,' said Patrick.

'Oh, what injustice! To think that I long for mine to ring just once.'

When they got out of the car Patrick said: 'Do you think we'll be needing it any more, Nicholas?'

'Oh do keep it, Patrick,' said Christopher. 'I'd love to go home in it. Just imagine what my friends would say when they saw me gliding along the Fulham Road.'

As they went up in the lift Patrick said: 'I hope you're not going to be disappointed. It's very simple and slightly *bourgeois*. But then I am.'

'Nonsense. You're almost aristocratic,' said Christopher. 'That's why sometimes I can't help hating you.'

'Don't say you want to chop off my head,' said Patrick. 'You'll protect me, won't you, Nicholas?'

While he was fitting the key into the lock, the telephone inside the flat began to ring.

'There it goes again! Answer it, Nicky. Say that I'm out.'

Nicholas picked up the receiver.

'Is Patrick there? Who's that speaking? It's Ronnie Gras here. I want to speak to Patrick.'

'Who is it?' called Patrick.

'Mr Gras.'

'Tell him I'm in my bath looking at some pictures I've just bought.'

Nicholas repeated the message.

'Buying pictures? What has he bought? How many?' Nicholas put his hand over the receiver. 'He wants to know how many pictures you've bought, Patrick.'

'Tell him a Matisse and an early Moore drawing.'

Nicholas heard Ronnie gasp. There was a click as the telephone was replaced.

'He sounded winded,' said Nicholas.

'Silly old chimp,' said Patrick. 'Do you know, my dears, I must be going out of my mind. I've suddenly remembered that I haven't an ounce of tea in the place.'

'May I mix a cocktail instead, Patrick?' said Christopher.

'Do anything you like while I drag myself out of this suit. I simply must have a bath. Make yourselves at home. But try not to do too much damage. Ronnie sat on my only Renoir last week.

And you know how much he weighs. I suppose it was rather careless of me to leave it lying in the most comfortable chair.'

Christopher giggled. He picked up the cocktail shaker.

'It's such fun mixing drinks here,' he said. 'There's absolutely everything. Even vodka.'

Michael examined the room. He counted ten pictures hanging on the walls. Others were propped on the tops of book-cases and on the mantelpiece. He took the glass that Christopher handed him and tasted the drink. 'What a revolting brew, Christopher,' he said.

Nicholas stood by the window looking out over the tops of the trees in the park opposite. He turned and faced the room admiring the thick white carpet, the Adam fireplace and the pictures. The cigarette burns on the edge of the Sheraton table worried him. He walked towards it and bent over it. Christopher put a glass in his hand.

Absentmindedly he raised it to his lips.

'Whatever have you put in it, Christopher?' he said.

'I said it was piss,' said Michael.

'I think it's terribly good,' Christopher said sulkily.

Nicholas went to the cupboard and poured himself a tomato juice. Carrying his glass with him he went into the hall to explore the flat. From the door to his left he could hear the sound of running taps. There was a faint smell of scent in the air.

'Is that you, Nicky?' called Patrick. 'Be an angel and go and put a record on. I think some Mozart would be rather gay. You'll find the machine in the bedroom.'

'Can I have a bath when you've finished?' said Nicholas.

'Of course. What would you like in it? I know. Something delicious and expensive.'

The long player stood on a table by the bed. The room was sparsely furnished. A narrow bed, a chair and a small Queen Anne bureau.

'In my lady's chamber, eh?' said Michael who had followed Nicholas into the bedroom. 'For God's sake put something lively on and jive this cell up a bit. Can't say I'd care to sleep here. Too bloody monastic for me. Do you think you'll be able to manage it?'

'Aren't you funny,' said Nicholas. He chose a record, put it on, and turned up the volume.

Patrick came into the room wearing a dressing gown of black silk.

'I've run your bath, Nicky, and put you out a big clean towel. My dear, this doesn't sound like Mozart to me! Never mind. It's a gay tune. Quite one of my favourites. I believe it was the rage of the 'twenties.'

'Then you should know it well,' said Michael.

Patrick said: 'Why don't you go and fill your glass?'

In the hall Nicholas said: 'I don't think that was necessary, Mike.'

'Come off it! I bet that rich old quean loves being hurt. If you beat him hard enough you might knock some of the boredom out of him.' He walked in to the sitting-room and picked up the bottle.

Nicholas went into the bathroom and locked the door. The bath was full and smelt strongly of scent. Along the shelf over the basin was a row of glass-stoppered bottles labelled with the names of trees: myrtle, bay, chestnut and cedar.

He took off his clothes and stepped into the bath. After he had bathed he would have to make an excuse and slip away. He certainly didn't want to spend the evening with Michael. He didn't like his insinuations. Patrick was a good friend of his and nothing more. He had no right to put such a nasty interpretation on their friendship. The trouble was that Michael was jealous. It was quite clear that he wasn't successful. As a result he resented anyone else's good fortune. More than likely he was furious that he wasn't going to start work on the *Gladiator* himself.

Patrick knocked on the door. 'Don't linger too long in the sandalwood,' he called.

Nicholas got out of the bath, dressed, and went back into the sitting-room.

'Can we all go out together?' Christopher said. 'It would be such fun. Where do you think the boys would like to eat, Patrick?'

'We could try the *Pelouse d'Or*. At least one knows that one can eat the food there,' said Patrick.

'How wonderful. It's the smartest restaurant in London!' said Christopher.

'Ring them up and reserve a table, Nicky,' said Patrick.

Nicholas looked up the number in the directory.

'I want a table for four, please.'

'I'm sorry. We have no tables left.'

Nicholas turned to Patrick. 'They're full up.'

'Tell them it's for me,' said Patrick.

Nicholas gave Patrick's name. He saw Michael grinning at him.

'Of course, sir. I'll reserve the usual table.'

'If only I could get tables like that,' said Christopher. 'I do envy you, Patrick. Don't you think it's marvellous to have such an open sesame, Nicky?'

'Yes, wasn't it clever of Nicky?' said Patrick. 'You're so good at this kind of thing that I'm sure you'll do just as well if you telephone the taxi rank.'

'What about your car?' said Christopher.

'How silly of me.'

When they were in the car Nicholas said: 'Do you think we could pick up my things and drop them at Chelsea Square before dinner?'

'If you mention your *things* again, I shall scream,' said Patrick. 'We can't possibly drag Christopher and Michael half way across London for one sad suitcase.'

'I could ride round and round in this car for ever. I don't mind where we go, Patrick,' said Christopher.

'You shall have it all to yourself tomorrow,' said Patrick. 'But we must eat now or poor Michael will die. I'm sure you don't feed him properly.'

The entire staff of the *Pelouse d'Or* seemed to converge upon them as they walked into the restaurant. The head waiter hurried forward and escorted them to their table.

'They seem to like you here, Nicky,' said Patrick. 'I suspect they know you're the star boy of the *Gladiator*. I'm sure very shortly you'll be dining and wining here on that fat expense account.'

Nicholas glanced at the menu that the head waiter placed in front of him. He hoped that Patrick didn't expect him to pay the bill.

'What an enormous selection. I don't know where to start. What are you going to have, Patrick?' he said.

'I'm dieting, my dear. So it will have to be the usual. Rice pudding.'

'What?'

'With a glass of milk of course. If you like rice pudding you shall have a spoonful of mine.'

'Patrick is really a saint,' said Christopher. 'He never eats anything. He's a natural ascetic. He's really living out of his time. He'd have made such a good desert father. If everyone was like Patrick I'm sure there would be less injustice in the world. On the other hand, we're not all born like him. Perhaps it's just as well. We suffer because of the excesses of the flesh. Without suffering we would never learn wisdom. I'm afraid if we all dieted on rice the world would never progress.'

'Oh goodness!' exclaimed Patrick.

'Have I said something terribly wrong?' said Christopher.

'Nicky, my dear, there's your boss,' said Patrick. 'The china-woman with him is his wife.'

Stuart saw Patrick, got up, and came over to the table.

'Hello, Oscar,' he said.

Nicholas stood up.

'Stuart, this is Nicholas Milestone. He tells me he's going to work for you,' said Patrick.

'How are you, son? Sit down. You'll get cramp standing.'

'Do you know Christopher Lyre, Stuart?' said Patrick.

'Lyre? Lyre? Of course. The painter johnny. Your stuff's not as degenerate as some muck I was looking at yesterday. I don't think we're having a go at you,' said Stuart.

'What a pity! I've always wanted to be in the news,' said Christopher.

'Not the way we're featuring your decadent pals,' said Stuart. 'We're going to get that exhibition closed in the interests of public morality. What do you make of that trash, son? Feel you could give it hell?'

'I don't know, sir,' said Nicholas.

'Better make up your mind quick.'

When Stuart had gone back to his own table Patrick said: 'How do you like your boss, my dear? So cultured, isn't he?'

'He's not really demanding that the exhibition should be closed?' said Nicholas.

'He spends his whole life demanding. I'm sure you'll be just as good at it,' said Patrick.

'I hope he doesn't expect me to write that kind of thing,' said Nicholas.

'You'll probably find you can do it just as well,' said Patrick. 'We'll all know that you won't really mean it.'

'That's what makes it so wicked,' said Christopher. 'None of them believes a word he writes. Nicky's much too nice for them. I think it's quite wrong that he should work for the *Gladiator*.'

'Nicky must make up his own mind,' said Patrick.

'Why don't you let him work for *Eleven*?' said Christopher.

'That would be entirely up to Ronnie. I keep telling you he's the editor, not I. Anyway we haven't even asked Nicky what he thinks about it.'

'He couldn't refuse,' said Christopher. 'In fact I think both he and Mike should work for *Eleven*. There's going to be masses to do. Nicholas can work on the literary side, and I'll find Mike a job with me. After all, Mike should be an artist. Just look at his hands.'

Soon after midnight they left the restaurant. While they were standing in the street waiting for the car to be brought round, Christopher said: 'Could you take us home, Patrick?'

'Oh dear, I feel I really ought to get Nicky to his room,' said Patrick.

'Of course you must. I'm afraid we'll have to walk, Mike,' said Christopher.

Patrick took Nicholas by the arm and helped him into the back of the Rolls. 'Tired, little one?' he said.

'Rather. I think I've drunk too much.'

'Good night, Nicholas old chap,' called Michael. 'Fly away in your great big car. Dirty old bus for me.'

Nicholas leant back against the thick upholstery and dozed. Patrick told the chauffeur to drive to the Rialto.

'All right, Nicky?' he asked. 'I think you'd better come up with me first and have an Aspirin. Then I'll pop you back in the car.'

When they reached the Rialto Patrick helped him out of the car, and guided him through the door and across the foyer.

In the lift Nicholas felt sick. When they went in to the bedroom the chandelier seemed to be swaying. He tried to focus his eyes, but objects continued to wallow in a deep swell.

'Perhaps a small brandy would be the best thing,' said Patrick.

He poured a small measure of brandy into a glass and handed it to Nicholas. 'You'd better sit down, my dear. I can see you're absolutely exhausted. You've had too much excitement for one day. It was very naughty of me to take you out this evening.'

Nicholas sat on the edge of the bed. He looked towards the pillows and noticed that his pyjamas had been laid out on top of the turned back sheets.

'They're my pyjamas, Patrick,' he said.

'I thought perhaps you'd better stay here the night. It's much too late to go chasing round London. It'll be so much easier for you to move in tomorrow.'

He walked across the room and sat down on the bed next to Nicholas.

'You smell of sandalwood,' he said.

'You smell nice too,' said Nicholas.

He stood up, steadied himself, and crossed the room to the dressing table. He started to empty his pockets. He took out his cigarette case. In his trouser pocket he felt something crinkly. A five-pound note.

He threw it on the table. It landed next to the gold case.

THREE

WHEN Michael woke he noticed that he had forgotten to open the window. The air in the room smelt stale. His mouth was dry. He got up from the divan, went into the bathroom, and let the water from the cold tap trickle into his mouth and down the sides of his face. The basin was coated with soap and toothpaste. Round the inside of the bath was a line of thick dirt.

He returned to the studio where Christopher was lying fully clothed on the sofa under the window. As Michael entered the room he turned over on to his side and opened his eyes.

'Hullo, Mike. Are you all right?'

'Shouldn't I be?'

'We drank rather a lot last night, I'm afraid. Shall I get up and make some tea?'

'It won't make itself.'

Christopher sat up. 'Oh dear, you're hating me this morning. I wish you wouldn't. Not so early anyway. I haven't any resistance before midday. One should try and love people in the morning.'

He slid his feet with their uncut and dirty nails into a pair of down-at-heel bedroom slippers. 'I'm afraid I'm not a very good host. This is really a workshop. It doesn't lend itself to entertaining.'

Michael looked round the studio. The mantelpiece was thick with dust. The fireplace was filled with rolled up pieces of paper and old cigarette packets. The bare boards were blotched with smears of paint. Stacks of canvases were piled against the walls.

'I suppose it's artistic,' he said. 'Not squalid enough though for a really great artist and hardly luxurious enough for a successful one.'

'You mustn't mock me like that, Mikey,' said Christopher. 'It's not easy to steer a middle course. I know what I ought to do, but I have to think about earning a living. It's terribly difficult to know how far one can compromise without losing one's integrity.

49

Sometimes I'm terrified to think that I may have gone too far, like Ronnie.'

'What about tea?'

Christopher shuffled into the kitchenette. Michael stood by the window and peered down into the Fulham Road. He tried to open the window but it was stuck. The sash had broken and the window had been screwed to the frame. Everything in the studio was the same. Neglected, chipped and dirty. The whole house was dropping to bits. Everywhere the dirt accumulated. Even the blankets on the divan were impregnated with smog. People sat on them, flicked ash over them, spilt drink on them, and then slept in them.

He looked at his portrait on the easel in the centre of the room. Did he really look like that? Bucolic and dumb. And those hands! His most interesting and compelling feature, Christopher kept saying.

He looked at his hands. They were as broad as they were long. His fingers reminded him of stubby pork sausages. Navvy's hands.

'There's no milk,' shouted Christopher. 'I suppose it's because I've forgotten to pay them. Can you drink it without or shall I try to borrow some?'

'Without.'

He continued studying the portrait. He had to admit that he liked it in spite of the accent on his hands. Everyone laughed at Christopher. But they had to concede the fact that he was a talented painter.

'I'm afraid I've broken the spout,' said Christopher. He put two cups and a bag of sugar on the sofa. As he poured the tea it dripped down the side of the pot.

'God, what squalor!' said Michael.

'Isn't it terrible?' said Christopher. 'I don't see how one can avoid it if one hasn't a woman in one's life. Women are terribly good at looking after houses and keeping them clean. Otherwise they're diabolical. They're so terribly possessive.'

'I didn't know you knew anything about women.'

'I was married once.'

'Good God! To whom?'

'Someone terribly good. She stayed with me as long as she could but in the end I drove her away. The trouble is that now I don't feel sorry about it, which must be very wicked of me. At the time I was terribly upset. I thought she should have understood that there is more than one kind of love. But I never even succeeded in convincing her that the nature of love is promiscuous and uncontrollable.'

'What happened, Christopher?'

'It's a silly story. The kind of thing that can happen to anybody like me. One day I met a guardsman. . . .'

'Where?'

'Outside Buckingham Palace. I felt terribly sorry for him. He wanted me to buy him out. I was too poor at the time, but in the end I persuaded Anna, that was the name of my wife, to lend me the money. So he came to live with us here. We adopted him as a son. But it wasn't a great success. Anna became terribly jealous and accused me of having incestuous relations with him. Do you see what I mean? He was our son. But I couldn't bring myself to turn him out. I painted some very good pictures of him. You may have seen them. Then one day Anna walked out on me.'

'What happened to the guardsman?'

'He walked out soon afterwards. He took all the silver with him. You mustn't think I minded about that. After Anna had gone there was no one left to clean it.'

The telephone started to ring. Michael picked it up.

'Good morning, Mike. How do you feel?' said Nicholas.

'Fine. How's the million-dollar baby this morning?'

'Who?'

'Sugar Daddy's new chum.'

'About meeting today. Would you like to lunch with me here at the Rialto?'

Michael let out a whistle. 'You've certainly got cracking! Do I put on my morning suit? Or isn't the wedding quite yet?'

'You're too brilliant for words this morning! How's the great painter treating you?'

'Christopher's been entertaining me with a slice of his life,' said Michael. 'I'll meet you about half-past twelve. Give my love to Daddy.' He put down the receiver.

'What's that about me?' asked Christopher.

'Nicky was asking after your health.'

'How nice of him. But then he's an awfully nice person. I feel frightened for him. He's in such terrible danger. As one of his oldest friends I think you ought to warn him.'

'So you think gold mining a dangerous pursuit?'

'Once you've decided to be a miner, you become incapable of doing anything else.'

'How long have you known Patrick?'

'I first met him when he was sharing a house with Ronnie Gras,' said Christopher. 'It's difficult to believe now, but in those days he was fascinated by Ronnie. That's probably the reason he's so nasty to him now. But he soon became bored with Ronnie as he does with everybody. I'm afraid it won't be long before he loses interest in this new magazine. He's going to break lots of hearts and set a whole series of new feuds and hates in motion.'

'You talk sense at times.'

'Do you really think so?'

'You talk so much that you can't help making an intelligent observation now and again in spite of yourself.'

'I hate you,' said Christopher. 'If you've finished breakfast I'd like to get on with some work while the light's good.'

He picked up his palette and started to mix the paints.

'Do we talk this morning?' asked Michael.

'Yes. I've passed the difficult phase. I've only got to give substance to the idea. Have you known Nicholas for long?'

'Since school.'

'He is a nice person, isn't he?'

'Do you want to paint him?'

'I'd like to help him if he's a friend of yours. He looks so sad. Those spaniel eyes upset me.'

'He was always professionally sad,' said Michael. 'Once upon a time he imagined himself a poet. But he didn't seem at all sad to me last night. He's riding on the crest of the wave I should say.'

'Poor boy. I wonder what'll happen to him.'

'Nicky's old enough to take care of himself.'

'But is he strong enough?'

'You don't seem to have a very good opinion of Patrick this morning,' said Michael.

'He's always teasing me,' said Christopher. 'He thinks I'm a fool. That's true in many ways. But it doesn't make being laughed at any less painful. You mustn't think I actively dislike him. I don't. I'm sorry for him. I can see the loneliness behind his rich exterior. The rich are the loneliest people in the world. They can never know the meaning of friendship. They think their friends only love them for their money.'

'If that's the way you feel, I can't see why you have anything to do with him.'

'I try to ignore the humiliations and tell myself it doesn't matter. It's far more important if I can persuade him to do something really worthwhile with his money. This magazine for instance.'

'Do you think he'll go ahead with it? Were you really serious last night when you said you thought Nicholas ought to work for it?'

'Of course. And what about you? Wouldn't you like to?'

'It's not my line. No, Chris. I'm no good at anything. Except flying. And that's outmoded. If there's another war they'll only want people who know which buttons to press.'

'You mustn't talk like that. It's suicidal. Nihilistic,' said Christopher. 'That's why I want you to stay with me until something inside you starts to germinate. I like having someone to help.'

'It must be wonderful to know what you want to do,' said Michael. 'Look at Nicholas. He's mad to start work on the *Gladiator*. The thought of doing something makes him forget what a load of muck he's letting himself in for.'

'It's a wicked paper. It plays on humanity's vices,' said Christopher.

'Do you think Nicholas is wicked to work for it?'

'I don't expect he has a choice. You see I'm not an existentialist. How could I be? No one has ever been able to explain it to me as a layman. Sometimes I think we have choice, but more often I feel we're like animals. We're motivated by desires and atavism.'

'What do you think of Stuart Andrews?'

'He's a disappointed intellectual. One of Patrick's protégés many years ago.'

'If Patrick turns Nicholas into anything as horrible, the devil won't have him in hell,' said Michael.

The door bell started to ring.

Christopher put down his brush, took a tie off the mantelpiece and twisted it round his neck, omitting to put it under his collar.

'If you've visitors, I'm going to shave,' said Michael.

The bell rang again. A voice from outside called: 'Must I wait all morning in the street, Christopher?'

Christopher ran down the stairs and opened the door.

'Hullo, Ronnie. I didn't expect you to come here at this hour of the morning.'

'This is Lily,' said Ronnie.

The girl who was clutching Ronnie's arm smiled at Christopher. 'I've heard a lot about you, Mr Lyre.'

'Can we come up?' asked Ronnie.

'If you want to. I didn't ask you to because you always refuse. I'm afraid it isn't any cleaner than usual.'

'Isn't there a lift in this place yet?' said Ronnie as they slowly climbed the stairs.

They went into the studio.

'Oh dear, I don't know where you can sit, Lily,' said Christopher. 'No. Not there. It's covered with sugar. Look, I'll spread a clean canvas on the divan.'

Ronnie was examining the picture on the easel. He put his face within two inches of the canvas.

'It could be good, Christopher,' he said at last. 'But I'm not sure if I approve of the application.'

'It's Michael Henry, you know. He's staying with me,' said Christopher.

'When did you last see Patrick?' asked Ronnie.

'He took us all out to dinner last night.'

'Where?'

'The *Pelouse d'Or.*'

'I hope you tried the pâté.'

'I'm afraid not. Did I miss something?'

Ronnie sighed and shook his head. 'Only the finest pâté in London. They have a tolerable cellar too. Wouldn't you agree, Lily?'

'Oh yes, Ronnie.'

'What did Patrick have to say for himself last night?' said Ronnie. 'It may interest you to know that he had made a tentative arrangement to dine with me.'

'I'm awfully sorry about that. It wasn't my fault. I promise you.'

'Never mind that. What did he talk about? Did he have much to say about my magazine?'

'As a matter of fact he spent most of the evening talking to Nicholas Milestone,' said Christopher.

'Just as I thought.'

'I can't see what you're getting at,' said Christopher. 'You needn't worry about Nicholas. He's terribly nice.'

'Indeed?'

Ronnie passed Christopher a sheet of writing paper. Christopher immediately recognized Patrick's handwriting.

'Dear Chimp,' he read, 'I decided after our chat this morning in favour of your little idea. It should be fun for you and good for your vanity at the same time. I think you *should* use Christopher as he's such a *popular* figure, especially after the success of his exhibition. But I leave this entirely to you. You must engage whom you like. In return I'd ask you to reserve a small niche for Nicholas. He'll be able to watch my interests as naturally I shall want to stay in the background. I enclose a little cheque for the first month. Financial matters will be in the hands of Messrs Warm & Warm. I believe you have had dealings with them before. They'll tell you how much, if any, I can afford to lose. I think it would be a good idea if you organized one of your charming little soirées at your palace. We could sit round and iron out any difficulties. The world whispers that you have bought some new oddments, and that the palace grows GRANDER day by day. That's if you don't mind having us. Love. PATRICK.'

'How wonderful!' exclaimed Christopher. 'He's really going to do it! I'm to be the art editor and you're to be my boss! You're not a slave driver are you, Ronnie?'

'Control yourself, please,' said Ronnie. 'Perhaps you can enlighten me. What exactly does he mean by "Dear Chimp"?'

'Is it a boxer? No, that's a champ.'

'Do I look like a pugilist?'

Christopher looked at the rolls of fat on Ronnie's neck and his protruding stomach.

'Slightly,' he said. 'But a terribly seedy one.' He giggled.

'Lily, it's time we went,' said Ronnie.

'I wasn't laughing at you,' said Christopher. 'I'm terribly sorry if you think I was. I'm sure Patrick didn't mean a thing. It's probably another of his silly private jokes.'

'Another gold-plated insult if you ask me,' said Ronnie. 'Now what's all this nonsense about Nicholas? Who is he anyway?'

'He's Patrick's new boy friend.'

'Does he imagine I'm editing a magazine for his current catamite?' said Ronnie.

'You shouldn't worry about Nicholas,' said Christopher. 'What really matters is that Patrick is prepared to finance you. He even sent you a cheque. Was it a large one?'

Ronnie ignored the question. 'I thoroughly disapprove of his flippancy,' he said. 'One should never jest with art. Besides, there's my reputation to be considered.'

'I'd forgotten that.'

'Patrick's got to take it seriously. I'm not going to have him lurking in the background causing trouble when he's got nothing better to do. If he says I can engage whom I want he's got to stick to that. I suppose the first thing he'll do will be to complain that I'm paying Lily too much.'

'I didn't know Lily . . .'

'I've got to have a secretary, haven't I?' said Ronnie. 'Quite apart from the question of your salary, Lily, you'd better be prepared for Patrick to start accusing you of trying to steal his latest protégé.'

'I wouldn't dream of doing such a thing,' said Lily.

'I should hope not.'

The door opened and Michael came into the studio.

'Michael, this is Lily,' said Christopher.

Michael crossed the room and shook hands.

'And this is Ronnie Gras.'

Michael nodded towards Ronnie. 'Ronnie who?'

'I'm Ronnie Gras.'

'I'm Michael Henry.'

'Michael's an old friend of Nicholas, Ronnie,' said Christopher.

Ronnie, who had started to walk towards the door, paused. 'How interesting. You've known him for some time then.'

'We were at school together.'

'Eton?' said Ronnie.

'Dartington.'

'Dartington? Dartington? That's a new school, isn't it? An extraordinary place where they do as they like. So you were there with young Milestone.'

'I was with him till they threw him out.'

'Thrown out of there!' exclaimed Ronnie. 'He must have behaved very badly indeed. A very peculiar young man, I should say.'

'He is,' said Michael. 'He's a wonderful knack of running into trouble. He makes a mess of whatever he does. I believe it's a failing of our generation.'

Ronnie had taken an instant dislike to Michael. He would have left but he did not like to miss the chance of learning more about Nicholas. If Nicholas was going to be thrown into close contact with him by Patrick, it was just as well to know as much about him as possible.

'What are young Milestone's plans at the moment?' he asked.

'He's got Patrick in a trance,' said Michael. 'Christopher of course thinks it's the other way round. But I expect you know much more about Patrick than I do. Perhaps you can tell me something. Do you think he'd pay well?'

'Pay whom?' said Ronnie.

'Me. After all, if I'm going to work for his magazine he won't expect me to do it for love.'

'But Mike, only a minute ago you said you didn't want to,' said Christopher. 'You see, Ronnie, I was talking to Michael about his future this morning and suggested we might be able to fit him in somewhere on *Eleven*.'

'With due respect to Mr Henry I would point out that *Eleven* is still in the embryo stage,' said Ronnie. 'Any appointments will be made by me. The sooner we clear these points up the better. I propose we meet at my house tomorrow as Patrick has suggested. Lily, what are my engagements for tomorrow?'

'You dine with Mr Toad at eight, dear,' she said.

'Call him and cancel it. Christopher, I'll expect you at my house tomorrow at seven. If possible in a clean suit. And try not to be late. Come, Lily, I'm sure it's getting on for lunch time. You know how long it takes you to find a cab at this hour of the morning.'

The footsteps on the stairs subsided. The front door banged. The shrill cries of Lily hailing a taxi floated up from the street.

'I'm so glad that you've decided to work on *Eleven* after all, Mike,' said Christopher. 'I'm sure you've made a wise decision. One so often finds that unpremeditated decisions are the best.'

'It was wonderful!' said Michael.

'What? Ronnie?'

'Her complexion. What a beautiful face,' said Michael.

'But she's terribly superficial. It's a face without a soul,' said Christopher.

'Who is she?'

'I only know that she's a friend of Ronnie,' said Christopher. 'He's terribly successful with women. It makes me quite jealous. I suppose that's why I never take to his girl friends. Jealousy's a terrible thing. One of the most destructive forces in the world. It blots out all perspective; makes people see reality through the haze of smoked glasses. If I really believed you thought Lily beautiful, I should lose all faith in you.'

'You'll have to lose it,' said Michael. 'Go ahead and be really miserable and have a thoroughly good time.'

'If that's how you feel, there's nothing I can say,' said Christopher. 'I feel like crying, that's all. I can't talk anyway when I'm crying.'

'Now I know what Anna had to put up with,' said Michael.

'She tried to understand and forgive me,' said Christopher. 'She certainly understood me as an artist if not as a man.'

'If I worked for *Eleven* I'd see a lot of Lily,' said Michael. 'She's much too beautiful for that slug Gras. What an incredible person he is! He treated her like dirt!'

'He treats them all like that,' said Christopher. 'He believes they like it. I think he's right. All women are masochists. After all, copulation is nothing more than the complete subjection of the female by the male.'

'I'm going out. I've had enough for one morning,' said Michael. 'I'll be back some time after lunch. While I'm out you might try and clean this place up a bit. And while you're about it, put on a clean shirt for God's sake.'

As Michael sauntered across the foyer of the Rialto he saw Nicholas coming out of the lift.

'All alone, Nicky?' he said. 'Where's your handy cheque book?'

'My what?'

'Patrick what's-his-name.'

'He's out shopping. Let's go and have a drink.'

'Here? It's ridiculously expensive.'

'I can afford it. Just this once.'

They went up the stairs into the bar and sat down at a table in the corner.

'I see you've been shopping too,' said Michael. 'I can't say I admire his taste.'

Nicholas fingered his new bow tie. 'If you must know I chose it myself. What's the matter with you this morning? Why do you keep getting at me?'

'I've had an illuminating conversation about you,' said Michael. 'I've decided to try to give you some advice. I know in advance that you're not going to thank me for it. I think now's a good time, seeing that the boy friend is out of the way.'

'Why don't you like Patrick?'

'He's charming. In his own way and with his own kind.'

'I know exactly what you're going to say.'

'I've already told you that you wouldn't thank me. You always were too bloody self-opinionated to take advice. You think you're a tough character. Actually you're softer than putty.'

'I know what I'm doing.'

'You haven't the faintest idea,' said Michael. 'You're not even in the professional class. You're just a pitiful amateur riding for one hell of a fall. How long do you think you're going to lounge

around this ritzy bar drinking champagne and looking pretty in
your new bow tie?'

'I should start work tomorrow.'

'*Should?* You don't sound very enthusiastic about it. Hadn't you
better make up your mind which career you're going to follow? I
imagine they're both profitable. But you've got to give your un-
divided attention to one or the other.'

'You're very wise this morning,' said Nicholas. 'But it's not very
impressive coming from you. What exactly are *you* doing?'

Michael laughed. 'Me? I don't matter. I've got nothing to
throw away. Christopher told me in one of his delightfully frank
moments that the best thing that could have happened to me was
to have been killed flying. When I first met him I rather despised
him because in those days I was doing something which he could
never do. Now he's got the laugh on me. I rather like him for it,
because in his stupid way he worries far more about me than I do
about myself. He thinks I'm suicidal. So I bought a gun to find
out.'

He took an automatic from his pocket and laid it on the table
beside his glass.

'For God's sake put it away. There'll be a hell of a row if anyone
sees it,' said Nicholas.

'I can't see why. I wouldn't dream of shooting myself here,' said
Michael.

'Does Christopher know you carry that about?'

'No. He'd be terribly excited if he did.'

'You're madder than I thought,' said Nicholas.

'Not mad. Just an idler and a potential criminal. But not mad.'

'Put it away, please. I'll order another drink.'

Michael picked up the automatic, wiped it with his handkerchief and slipped it back in his pocket.

'Would you like to lunch at the *Pelouse d'Or*?' asked Nicholas.

'Wherever you like. You're paying.'

Ten minutes later they left the bar. As they went down the stairs
Michael said: 'I can see you like it here. It means something to you.
If this is what you want you'd better make up your mind and go all
out for it. If you try half measures you'll lose the lot.'

They walked in silence down Piccadilly.

Nicholas resented Michael's attempt to intrude into something which did not concern him. It was all very well for Michael to pretend to be altruistic. It was far more likely that he was jealous. He was, after all, just another misfit. One read about them every day in the papers. They were becoming rather bores. As far as he himself was concerned, if Patrick wanted to give him a good time, he would be a fool to throw it back in his face. Pleasure was harmless. Only Puritans condemned it out of hand. And he certainly had no time for Puritans.

Michael didn't give Nicholas another thought. He had said all that he intended to say. The only person who interested him now was Lily. How had someone as hideous as Ronnie managed to get hold of someone so beautiful? He would certainly go tomorrow to Ronnie's house with Christopher. The prospect of seeing Lily again was exciting. In any case it would be amusing to see Patrick holding court, surrounded by a pack of sycophants all trying to wheedle something out of him.

The *Pelouse d'Or* was crowded.

'My God! Look over there!' said Michael. 'Patrick. Lunching with your boss.'

Nicholas was embarrassed. Patrick had said nothing to him about coming to the *Pelouse d'Or* for lunch.

'Let's go into the bar and have a drink,' he said. 'I don't understand Patrick at all. I suppose one mustn't be surprised if one sees him dining with Farouk.'

On the way to the bar they were met by the head waiter. 'Good morning, gentlemen. Will you be joining Mr Andrews and Mr . . . ?'

'We're going to have a drink first,' said Nicholas. 'But I shall want a separate table. A table for two.'

They walked through the restaurant and sat down on stools at the bar.

Patrick and Stuart got up from their table and walked towards them.

'I thought it was you,' said Patrick. 'How clever of you to find it again. You must like it here.'

'I'm giving Michael lunch,' said Nicholas.

'Quite right too. Never be mean to your friends.' He leant over, so that Nicholas could smell his scent. 'Are you *sure* you've enough money? Your friend *drinks* rather a lot, I believe.'

Michael heard Patrick distinctly. Nicholas almost pushed him away: 'Plenty, thank you, Patrick.'

'Sure?' he insisted.

'Of course.'

Stuart took Patrick's arm and led him back to the table.

'I don't know which I dislike the most now,' said Michael. 'I'm sorry for you on both accounts.'

'I don't think Mr Andrews recognized me,' said Nicholas. 'After all we only met for the first time last night.'

Nicholas knew that he wasn't going to enjoy his lunch when he found that they had been placed at a table in full view of Patrick, who was chatting happily to Stuart. Occasionally Stuart would say something and Patrick would lean back against the red plush and shake with laughter.

'Your lunch may be ruined. Mine isn't,' said Michael. 'Can't you take your eyes off him for one minute? He won't run away.'

Nicholas didn't find conversation with Michael easy. He regretted having asked him to lunch. He was a bore and rather a coarse one at that. If Patrick had suddenly decided to lunch with the editor of the *Gladiator* that was his own affair. Still, it was strange that he hadn't so much as mentioned it.

Stuart stood up, called for his coat, and walked out of the restaurant.

Patrick raised his finger and beckoned to Nicholas.

'He wants us to join him,' said Nicholas.

They left their own table and walked across the room.

'Did you have a delicious lunch?' asked Patrick.

'Not very,' said Nicholas.

Patrick took him by the elbow and pulled him down beside him on the banquette.

'Then we must find somewhere better for you this evening,' he said.

'I don't feel much like going out.'

'What have you been doing to him, Michael? You've made him positively grumpy.'

'I'm not grumpy,' said Nicholas. 'I just meant the lunch wasn't very good. There wasn't enough of it.'

'Then you must have another one,' said Patrick.

'I'm not hungry.'

'If you haven't had enough you must be hungry, my dear,' said Patrick.

He summoned the waiter.

'Oysters? Caviare? Champagne? Would they cheer you up?'

'I've told you. I don't want anything.'

'A little pâté perhaps?'

'Please, Patrick.'

'As you wish, my dear. I'm only trying to tempt you. What about you, Michael? I know you'd like a drink. What about coffee and brandy?'

He picked up the wine list and studied it.

'Such charming names! *Charles Dix*. How would that be?'

'Whatever you say, Patrick,' said Nicholas.

'So you're going to join us. That's wonderful news. Then I say *fine champagne* and apricot brandy for me.'

There was silence at the table. The coffee was brought and the glasses placed in front of them. Nicholas stirred his coffee. Michael turned in his chair and stared round the restaurant.

'You two are sad,' said Patrick. 'I'd so hoped you might be able to cheer me up. Stuart was such a bore at lunch. That reminds me, Michael. Would you ring him when you've got the time.'

'Me?'

'Yes. You, dear. You are the friend of Nicky's who used to play with aeroplanes, aren't you? I'm sure Nicky said so.'

'What's that got to do with the editor of the *Gladiator*?'

'He mentioned something about a charter company. Freighters, whatever they may be. Some idea of flying his scandal sheet round the world. I honestly didn't really understand what he was talking about. If you want to know more, you'll have to ask him to explain.'

'Did he mention me?' said Nicholas.

'I'm afraid not. Should he have done?'

The waiter placed two bills on the table.

'Which is yours, Nicky?' said Patrick. 'The big one or the small one? Let's have a look. Six martinis and a bottle of wine. I didn't drink a bottle of wine, and I wouldn't dream of braving six martinis. I'm afraid the large one is yours.' He took out a pencil and signed his own bill.

Nicholas examined his own bill carefully.

'Anything wrong?' said Patrick. 'I do hope they haven't overcharged you.'

'It seems a terrible lot,' said Nicholas.

'What shall we do about it? I know. Just sign it. It's so much cheaper.'

He held out his pencil. Nicholas took it and held it poised above the bill. He looked up and saw Patrick smiling at him.

'Just sign. It's terribly simple.'

Nicholas signed the bill.

'That wasn't very painful, was it?' said Patrick. He picked up the bill. 'What funny writing. I wonder if they'll be able to read it? Perhaps we'd better make it absolutely clear.'

He signed his own name across Nicholas's signature.

They left the restaurant and walked out into the street.

'Thank you for lunch, Patrick,' said Michael.

'You must thank Nicholas,' said Patrick.

'I expect I'll see you tomorrow evening, Nicholas,' said Michael. He turned and walked away.

When he had disappeared round the corner Patrick said: 'That's that. Now home for us, I think. You look tired, my dear. I'm sure an hour on your back with your feet up would be very good for you.'

In the taxi on their way to the Rialto Nicholas said: 'Why don't you like Michael, Patrick?'

'I think he's quite charming. You do say the funniest things. It's not his fault if he's just a trifle *gauche*.'

'It's awfully difficult to know what you're really thinking, Patrick,' said Nicholas.

FOUR

'IT's so much easier to take a Fortnum's hamper,' said Patrick. 'Besides, I never could cut sandwiches.'

'The knife always charges off the wrong way,' said Nicholas. 'Everyone gets cross and says one's ruined the loaf.'

'I hate practical people,' said Patrick. 'You're delightfully impractical. That's why I like you.'

'Do you?' said Nicholas. He threw the crust off his slice of game pie into the water. The minnows swarmed round it.

'Of course I do, Nicky. Is there anything the matter? Aren't you enjoying yourself? How selfish of me. I keep forgetting that you've only just escaped from the country. Here I am dragging you back to it. You'd much rather have spent the day in London.'

Nicholas wondered if the moment had come when he could broach the subject that had been worrying him ever since they had driven down to Virginia Water. So far, whenever he had made the attempt Patrick had changed the conversation. He didn't know how to begin. He didn't want to put it as crudely to Patrick as he did to himself. He could hardly say: 'I'm worried about my future. How do I stand financially? I've no money of my own. I can't ask you for money every time I want to buy a box of matches. I want to know whether you're going to offer me a job on *Eleven* or not. I should have started work on the *Gladiator* today. I haven't in the belief that you would offer me something more attractive. If you don't, I've landed myself in a terrible mess.'

He threw another piece of crust into the water.

'What are you thinking about?' asked Patrick.

'The future.'

'Just look at those fish. They're making quick work of that pie. That's exactly how I sometimes feel. Nibbled at by greedy little fish with very sharp teeth. Do throw them some more.'

'It's all finished.'

'Would they like a peach?'

'No.'

'Not even Fortnum's?'

He threw the peach into the water. It bobbed up and down. The minnows ignored it.

'You're absolutely right, my dear. They won't even look at it. How did you know?'

'I used to fish.'

'How exciting! Tunny? Sharks? My dear, you're not big enough. They'd have pulled you into the water. I'd love to know how to fish.'

'Would you?' said Nicholas. He took a cigarette out of his case.

'How boring of me!' said Patrick. 'We were talking about the future. The future. That's rather an important time.'

'I wish you'd be serious, Patrick.'

'That's what Ronnie's always saying to me. If we're going to be in time for his dinner party tonight we ought to start making our way back to the car. I'm rather looking forward to this evening.'

'I'm not surprised. I think *Eleven* is a very exciting idea.'

'I'm not excited about that. It's the dinner I'm looking forward to,' said Patrick. 'When you dine with Ronnie you get some idea of what a banquet in Imperial Rome must have been like. It's so fantastically grand that one never dares to ask him to one's own house in return. Where he gets the money to pay for such feasts I simply can't imagine. If I even *thought* of living the way he does I should be in the bankruptcy courts within a week. Aren't you all agog at the prospect of tasting five different kinds of pâté, and drinking from the best cellar in England?'

'Not particularly.'

'You are in the doldrums. I know there's something worrying you. How am I going to persuade you to tell me what it is? I promise if it's a secret I won't tell a soul. After all, we can't have a glum face on *Eleven*, can we?'

'What do you mean?'

Nicholas was unable to conceal his eagerness.

'I'm sure I told you,' said Patrick. 'Or didn't I? I'm such a scatterbrain. It must have been Christopher I was talking to. Come a little bit closer and I'll whisper in your ear. That's better. And remember I won't take no for an answer.'

He began to stroke the back of Nicholas's neck.

'How delicious you feel there! Just like the muzzle of a pony. So soft and cuddly. I was talking to Christopher last night. He thinks it would be very wicked of you if you went to work on the *Gladiator*. I quite agree with him. But I didn't know what else you could do, until Christopher made the brilliant suggestion that you should work for *Eleven*. Don't you think that's a wonderful idea? If you find it too boring you can always change your mind and go on to the *Gladiator* later. Christopher thinks you might gain some very useful experience on *Eleven*. It'll give you time to find your feet and show us all exactly what you can do.'

'What did Ronnie have to say?'

'He doesn't know yet. I'll let you into a secret. I've made an alliance with Christopher. I think together we shall be able to overcome any opposition from Ronnie. I'm going to support his candidate if he supports mine.'

'His candidate?'

'Michael. Your dear old school chum.'

'What on earth will he do? I'm terribly fond of him, but honestly I don't see him fitting in on a magazine like *Eleven*.'

'That's Christopher's problem, my dear. You sounded almost jealous. I do hope you aren't. I thought it would be fun for you to have Michael working with you.'

'Of course it will. Thank you very much, Patrick.'

'What a funny thing to say. I haven't done a thing. Now you must tell me what's been worrying you all day.'

'Don't you see . . .' began Nicholas. He stopped. There was no longer any need to tell the truth. It would be far too embarrassing. 'Don't you see,' he lied, 'I've been desperately worried about Michael. He's my oldest friend, as you say.'

Patrick said: 'You must be devoted to him if that's what's made you such a crosspatch.'

'I am. I can't bear seeing him so unhappy. He's so bitter against everything and everyone.'

'Then we must do all we can to cheer him up,' said Patrick.

'I'm sorry to bore you,' said Nicholas.

'On the contrary, I think it's most touching.'

Nicholas decided that he'd better change the subject. He knew that he hadn't fooled Patrick. Patrick knew perfectly well that he had been thinking about himself all day; that he hadn't given Michael so much as a thought.

He stood up and brushed the crumbs off his trousers.

'Shall we start walking back?' he said.

'I'll show you a wonderful view of Belvedere,' said Patrick. 'It's not at all a bad house. The lake looks heavenly from the top windows.'

They walked in silence along the footpath.

'There! Look along that avenue of trees. Isn't it divine?' said Patrick.

'What did you mean about the view from the windows? Do you mean to say you've actually stayed here?'

'I'm afraid so. Years ago. Do you mind? . . . Now how do we get across this nasty puddle?'

Nicholas let go of his arm and jumped across it.

'How athletic! Do you think I could do that?' said Patrick.

'You'd better walk round.'

'One must never walk round anything. One must always keep straight ahead,' said Patrick.

He jumped and landed in the centre of the pool of rainwater. The muddy water splashed his socks and the bottoms of his trousers.

He held out both hands towards Nicholas. 'You'll have to be gallant, my dear. Come and rescue me.'

Nicholas opened his eyes as the car turned off the Great West Road and began to crawl on account of the traffic. Patrick was still sleeping, his hands resting on the newspapers which lay on his lap. He had drawn his trousers up and Nicholas could see splashes of mud on his socks.

The car stopped with a jerk as the traffic lights changed. Patrick opened one eye and winked at Nicholas.

'Not sleepy, Nicky?' He sat up on the seat. 'I've just had a delicious dream about you. Perhaps you aren't tired. What a tremendous amount of energy you have. I can't imagine where you find it. We'll have tea as soon as we get back. Then we shall have to start thinking about getting ready for Ronnie's ball. But you're not to eat too much tonight. You must think of your figure, my dear.'

'Who's going to be there?'

'Us. Christopher and Michael. And, of course, Ronnie's slave girl.'

'Who's she?'

'*Rather* attractive. At least Michael finds her so. He's a man, so he should know.'

'I don't believe it.'

'I'm afraid you're wrong, my dear. I've my own little secret sources. Don't ever be naughty and forget it. Your friend's crazy about her. If Ronnie finds out I don't think he'd be very pleased.'

As they went into the Rialto Nicholas said: 'Thank you for a lovely day, Patrick. I can't tell you how much I've enjoyed it.'

'But you are telling me. We must do it often if you like it. I was rather worried earlier because you didn't seem to find it amusing. But now I know what your trouble was I feel much better. We must make lots of expeditions. We might even go to Paris next week-end. Would you like that?'

'Very much.'

'Then we must keep it in mind. We might even go for longer. I don't know what you feel about the Rialto, but I'm beginning to get just a little tired of it. It's far too much like living on the *Queen Elizabeth*.'

He unlocked the door of the suite and went straight to the bedroom where he sat on the edge of the bed and took off his socks.

'Nicky, there's a parcel of socks from America on the table. Bring them in, will you?' he called.

Nicholas picked up the parcel and carried it into the bedroom.

Patrick was looking at his toes. 'Aren't they funny?' he said. 'I can't move the small ones at all, they're so deformed. Can you move yours?'

'I don't know.'

'Come and try.'

'I'm rather dirty. I think I'll bath.'

'But I love dirt. *So paysan*. Now off with your shoes and socks and show me your pretty little toes.'

'It's silly, Patrick. Suppose someone came in. They'd think us mad if they saw us sitting on the bed trying to move our little toes.'

'But they're charming toes. They'd be very lucky to see them.'

Nicholas sat down on the bed.

'I'll be your slave boy,' said Patrick. He knelt on the carpet in front of Nicholas and started to unlace his shoes.

'Let me do that,' said Nicholas. He tried to stand up but Patrick held him by the ankles as he knelt at his feet. Behind him Nicholas could see the soles of his feet and beyond them his muddy socks lying on the floor.

'Please, Patrick. Let me go,' he said. 'Please,' he repeated.

Patrick relaxed his grip, and sat back on his haunches. Nicholas saw him frown.

'I'm not detaining you, funny one. You are particular about your toes.'

He stood up, went to the mirror, and combed his hair. He hoped that his annoyance had not shown. But really, Nicholas was too extraordinary for words. What did he think he was playing at? In the mirror he could see Nicholas standing by the window about to take a cigarette out of his case.

'I wish you wouldn't smoke in here,' he said. 'Smoking in bedrooms is utterly barbaric.'

Nicholas was startled by the tone of Patrick's voice. He put the cigarette back in his case. It had not been a request but a command.

'I'm going to bath and change,' said Nicholas.

Patrick leant towards the mirror until he could feel the cool touch of the glass against his nose. He had bungled the scene but that didn't soften the blow to his vanity. It was no good pretending that he was still young. Age was an inevitability that had to be faced. He didn't expect young men to be attracted by his looks any more. But there was no reason why they shouldn't be nice to him for his money. That's to say, if they were going to reap the benefit of it. Nicholas didn't seem to have understood the position. He might be under the delusion that he was indispensable. Perhaps he didn't know that young men were like pictures you wanted to buy. You determined your top price. Beyond that you were not prepared to bid. Quite often you bought them well below your price.

Nicholas had a thoroughly miserable bath. He knew that he couldn't evade Patrick's advances much longer. It was no good pretending that Patrick was going to support him from purely altruistic motives. Patrick wanted his pound of flesh, he was going to make sure that he got it. What did sex matter anyway? It was a small price to pay for all the things that Patrick could offer him in exchange.

He got out of his bath, dressed quickly and went back into the sitting-room.

Patrick who had changed into a dinner jacket was sitting in front of the fire reading the evening paper.

'Feel cleaner?' he asked without looking up.

'I'm awfully sorry, Patrick.'

'Sorry? Sorry? How strange you are. What can there be to be sorry about? Come and sit by me and let me have a look at you.'

Nicholas sat down next to him and leant over to kiss him.

'No, no,' said Patrick. He pushed Nicholas away. 'I want to *look* at you. Yes, I like that tie. It brings out the bloom on your face. Pale blue and rosy cheeks go so well together. I feel you're going to be the belle of the ball tonight, my dear.'

'May I smoke?'

'Of course. I think I'll have one too.'

As Nicholas held a match to Patrick's cigarette, he congratulated himself on having so quickly restored the peace.

'Shouldn't we be going soon?' he asked.

'My dear, I forgot to tell you. You'll have to go on alone. I've a little visit to pay. I think you'd better warn Ronnie that I may be a little late.'

'Couldn't I wait for you? I don't know Ronnie. It's going to be rather embarrassing arriving without you.'

'You can always talk to Michael. I'm sure you've masses to tell him. You can take the car if you like.'

'How will you get there?'

'By bus. Are you all right for money? I don't think you'll need any but it's just as well to take precautions.'

'I've got plenty.'

'You'd better have some more. I think you'll find some on my dressing table. There's nothing more terrifying than being stranded without a penny, is there?'

Nicholas went into the bedroom. He wondered how much he was expected to take. All he could see on the dressing table was a heap of loose change lying among the powder dust and bottles. He opened the drawers in the hope of finding Patrick's note case but all he found were more bottles. He scooped up the money and counted it. It came to thirty shillings and fourpence.

When he went back into the sitting-room Patrick said: 'Did you find it?'

'I found some odd change.'

'Oh, it's not enough. I can see that you expected more. How mean of me.'

'It's plenty.'

'Nonsense,' said Patrick.

He went to the desk, took out his cheque book and wrote one out. He came back to Nicholas waving it in the air to dry the ink.

'There we are! I'm sure they'll cash it for you downstairs if you ask them *nicely*. But you've got to be nice about these things. Now run along and make my excuses to the Chimp.'

Nicholas took the cheque. Without looking at it he put it in his pocket. It was not until he was going down in the lift that he took it out to see how much it was for. He knew at once there was something wrong with it. Pay fifty pounds. But there was no signature at the bottom.

For one moment he thought he would take it back to Patrick and ask him to sign it. Patrick was upstairs waiting for him to come running back to beg him to put his magic mark on a piece of paper. He wouldn't go back. He'd been humiliated enough already for one evening. He might lose his temper. It would be wiser to keep out of Patrick's way.

He tore the cheque into shreds and dropped them into an ash tray.

As Nicholas was being driven in the Rolls to Ronnie's house he wondered if he had been wrong about the cheque. Perhaps Patrick had made a genuine mistake. It was stupid to have torn the cheque up in a fit of rage. He'd now have to think out some likely story. He could always say that he hadn't wanted to trouble Patrick and had destroyed the cheque because he was frightened of losing it. Someone might have picked it up and forged a signature. He could even say that he'd decided that it was wrong to take money that he didn't really need.

The beam of the headlights swung along the curve of the crescent and the car drew slowly to a halt outside the house. The chauffeur came round and opened the door.

Nicholas saw Ronnie standing at the top of the steps.

'Good evening, Patrick,' called Ronnie.

Nicholas got out of the car. 'I'm afraid Patrick's not here,' he said. 'He asked me to apologize and say he'd be a little late.'

'You'd better come in,' said Ronnie. 'What an extraordinary person Patrick is! What on earth has he found to do at this time of the evening?'

Nicholas followed Ronnie into the hall in the centre of which hung one of the largest crystal chandeliers that he had ever seen. Beneath it, standing on an ebony base, was the life-size statue of a man.

'How wonderful!' he exclaimed.

Ronnie did not know whether Nicholas was referring to the chandelier or the statue. But he was delighted by the unconcealed admiration in Nicholas's voice. 'Go and warm yourself by the fire,' he said. 'Lily will look after you.' He called out to her.

Lily came running out of the drawing-room.

'This is Mr Milestone, Lily. Take him into the drawing-room and give him a drink.'

'Yes, dear,' she said.

Nicholas followed her across the hall. In the drawing-room he went to the fire and held his hands towards the flames.

'You're a friend of Michael, I believe,' said Lily.

'I've known him for a long time.'

He watched her cross the room to the table and remove the

stopper from a decanter. She was small, and looked quite lost among the Empire furniture.

'Do you know Michael?' he asked.

'Oh, no. I only met him for the first time yesterday at Christopher Lyre's studio. Do you know Christopher's work? Ronnie calls it evasive.'

She handed Nicholas a glass of sherry.

'I hope you'll like it,' she said. 'Ronnie has it specially imported.'

'Lily!' called Ronnie from the hall.

'Excuse me a minute,' she said. 'Ronnie wants me. Coming, dear!'

Left alone Nicholas examined the room. As he had entered he had immediately been conscious of its size. He walked to the windows that overlooked the street. The thick velvet curtains had already been drawn. He turned and looked towards the door, and realized that the room was even vaster than he had first supposed.

Lily returned with Christopher and Michael.

'Hullo, Nicky,' called Christopher. 'Isn't it a palace? It's the only private house in London where you can still lose yourself. Hasn't Ronnie got the most wonderful taste? Where's Patrick? Is he playing hide and seek with you down there?'

Ronnie came in and sank down on the sofa in front of the fire. 'Sherry for Christopher, Lily,' he said. 'And a glass for Michael too.'

'Yes, dear.'

She poured out the sherry and carried round the glasses.

'Biscuits,' said Ronnie.

'Oh dear, I've left them in the pantry.'

Ronnie sighed.

'The sherry's terribly good without them, Ronnie,' said Christopher. 'Let me get them for you, Lily.'

'Do sit down before you knock something over, Christopher,' said Ronnie. 'Lily much prefers to run her own house. Don't you dear?'

'Yes, Ronnie. Shall I put the oysters on ice at the same time?'

Ronnie looked at his watch. 'Let me see. Provided Patrick arrives within the next twenty minutes no harm would be done. You can take the temperature of the burgundy at the same time.

But do it gently. On no account must it be disturbed. And if the pâtés are not absolutely firm, stand them in iced water.'

'Isn't he wonderful, Mike?' said Christopher. 'I don't know how you can care so much about food, Ronnie. I should love to be a perfectionist like you. I think your new statue's the most perfect thing I've ever seen in my life. Do tell me all about it.'

While Christopher and Ronnie were talking Michael put down his glass and followed Lily into the hall. She turned round and looked at him in surprise.

'Can I help you?' he asked.

'Oh, no. There's absolutely nothing to do.'

'I don't believe it.'

'I think you ought to stay with the others.'

Michael watched her as she disappeared through the door at the end of the hall before returning to the drawing-room.

'I can't imagine what Patrick's up to,' said Ronnie. He got up from the sofa and stood with his back to the fire looking at his watch.

'I'm sure he does lots of things that he never tells us about,' said Christopher.

'That's nothing to do with it. Manners and food are more important than anything else in the world.'

He turned to Nicholas. 'Didn't he give you any idea of where he was going? Are you sure he's coming at all?'

'He just told me to tell you he'd be a little late,' said Nicholas.

'But he knows I'm giving this dinner for him,' said Ronnie.

'If he doesn't come there'll be more for us, won't there, Ronnie?' said Christopher.

Ronnie ignored him. 'If he doesn't come soon everything will spoil. We can't decide a thing without him. Oh, he can be so infuriating!'

'I believe it's your fault, Nicholas,' said Christopher. 'You've upset Patrick. What have you done to him? It's no good denying it. I can see it in your eyes. They always betray people. They're such sensitive organs that they can't lie.'

'Lily,' called Ronnie. 'Lily.'

'I'll fill the glasses,' said Michael.

Ronnie appeared not to hear him.

They waited in silence listening to the sound of Lily's footsteps as she ran across the hall.

'Yes, dear?' She stood in the doorway, slightly out of breath.

Ronnie pointed to his glass. 'The guests first,' he said.

She carried the decanter round and filled the glasses. When she came to Ronnie she said anxiously, 'Is it all right? Or do you want me to bring you some from the other bin?'

Ronnie did not reply. He cocked his head to one side. 'I think I heard a car. Go and see if it's Patrick.'

She walked down the room. Michael reached the windows first and drew back the curtain.

'It's a taxi,' he said.

'Shall I answer the door, dear?' said Lily.

Ronnie shook his head and hurried out of the room.

Michael who was still standing next to Lily by the windows said: 'I'm afraid we're giving you an awful lot of trouble. We're rather a crowd to feed at such short notice.'

'Ronnie loves large dinner parties,' she said.

'Nicholas, didn't you tell Ronnie I'd be a few minutes late?' said Patrick as he came into the room. 'He seems almost angry with me.'

'A glass of sherry for Patrick,' said Ronnie.

Lily left Michael and hurried to the table.

'No, no. Let me do it,' said Patrick. He picked up the decanter. He filled his glass and went to the fire. 'What on earth's that new rock in the hall, Ronnie?' he said. 'He doesn't look at all happy under that chandelier. He's much too naked for all that light. I think it's rather naughty, my dear.'

'Don't say that, Patrick,' said Christopher. 'There's nothing obscene about it at all. It's only since we've lost our acceptance of the natural that we've begun to think in terms of obscenity. Don't you agree, Ronnie? After all, classically there's no such thing as obscenity.'

'You've got me wrong. I think it's a very proper piece of sculpture. I find it a little overpowering, that's all,' said Patrick.

Nicholas went to speak to Michael who was standing outside

the circle gathered round the fire. Ronnie started to expound the necessity for a classical revival in an age of mass production.

'What a pig!' said Michael. 'Just look at him!'

'I rather like him,' said Nicholas.

'I can't stand the way he treats that poor girl.'

'That's none of our business.'

'I'll lose my temper and tell him exactly what I think of him before the evening's out.'

'For God's sake don't be such a fool. I've got to create a good impression even if you haven't.'

'What are you two whispering about?' said Christopher. 'You should both be paying attention to Ronnie.'

'Indubitably that is why Colchester natives must rank among the peers,' said Ronnie. 'Their beds are well cultured, and there still lingers in them some flavour of their Roman progenitors.'

'Are we having them tonight, Ronnie?' asked Patrick.

'Naturally. Lily, I think we're now ready to go in.'

He took Patrick's arm and led the procession through the hall towards the dining-room. Patrick paused to look at the statue. 'I think we should take him in with us, Ronnie. He looks so lonely.'

'I fear he'd hardly be able to appreciate the bivalve mollusc,' said Ronnie.

'Slightly crustaceous tonight, aren't we?' said Patrick.

Christopher giggled and whispered to Michael: 'Aren't they clever? All those long words! I feel like a small boy being allowed to stay up for dinner as a special treat.'

Nicholas was amazed at the splendour of the dining-room. The long table glittered with glass and silver.

Ronnie walked slowly to the head of the table where Lily was waiting for him behind the high-backed chair. When he had seated himself she helped him ease the chair towards the table.

'Comfortable, dear?' she said. She picked up his napkin, unfolded it, and tucked it under his chin.

Ronnie watched her anxiously as she carried the salver packed with ice and oysters from the sideboard, and placed it before him. He leant forward and sniffed them. He frowned as he noticed a piece of weed protruding from the lip of one of them. He put out his hand, removed it with a look of intense displeasure, and handed it to Lily. He carefully placed a dozen oysters on a plate which Lily took and laid in front of Patrick. After he had helped himself he nodded to Lily. She picked up the salver and carried it to the lower end of the table.

'I would suggest a little Chablis, Patrick,' said Ronnie.

'My dear, there are so many glasses in front of me that I don't know where to start,' said Patrick.

'I can promise you this is Chablis. I would dare to boast that there's nothing comparable with it in the whole country at the moment.'

He steadied the bottle with his hand, and carefully wiped the lip with a clean napkin.

'This as you see is from the Pointes de Preuses. Perhaps the finest of all the vineyards. Although at times I must confess my loyalty wavers towards Valmur.'

He poured a little into his glass and held it against the candle-light, examining it critically. He drew the glass to his nose, and finally to his lips. He filled Patrick's glass and his own, and handed the bottle to Lily to take round the table.

'I must beg you all to look at the colour,' he said. 'Remark the pure paleness of the amber with its suspicion of green. That is Chablis. What frauds are committed in thy name!'

The dinner progressed. Before each course Ronnie delivered a short historical résumé of what they were about to eat. He enumerated the special virtues of each dish, paying particular attention to the joy that they brought to the mind as well as the palate. While he talked he never stopped eating.

Nicholas was astounded by the way Ronnie managed to concentrate on what he was saying and at the same time keep pace with his guests. Christopher was shocked at the amount that Ronnie consumed. The faces of starving children began to haunt him. But after he had drunk four glasses of wine he began to feel happier. He kicked Michael under the table as Ronnie began to elucidate some particularly contentious point concerning the breeding habits of bisexual mussels.

Patrick enjoyed himself enormously. He had been bidden to

Ronnie's table a sufficient number of times to know how he was expected to behave. He had to listen. The only time he had to talk was when the conversation showed signs of lagging and a new train of thought had to be supplied. Ronnie was at his very best. Patrick was delighted to notice that no one dared to interrupt him. It amused him to know that the extraordinary creature at the head of the table with the physiognomy of an ape and a mind of the most intricate and delicate pattern, was in a large measure one of his own creations.

'You must choose a small vineyard,' said Ronnie. 'That will help you to minimize the danger of disappointment. When you first visit it be sure that it is all Pinot. Not that the Gamay is always to be despised because it's afraid of the dark cellar. Now this vineyard of Richebourg. How big is it? Twelve or thirteen acres. Small, you see. But what is so supremely important, the property of one man. So we can be certain that every bottle that comes out of those sacred acres will be of the same superlative quality.'

'I thought one drank wines by the year, Ronnie,' said Christopher.

'A misconception. Or should I say a partial truth? Better a good wine of a bad year than a bad wine of a good one. To retrace our steps to burgundy. There's no doubt at all that too much favour has been showered upon Chambertin. If you will wander but a little farther into the adjoining commune of Morey-St-Denis, there in the Clos de Tart I would be so bold as to say that you will discover a wine incomparably finer.'

Lily placed the finger bowls on the table. Ronnie washed his mouth and removed the particles of food sticking to his fingers. She took the napkin from his neck and dropped it in a basket that stood beneath the sideboard.

Ronnie got up from the table, steadying himself with a hand on the edge.

'I think we'll have brandy in the drawing-room,' he announced.

'I thought the correct thing to do was to stay here, drink too much port and tell dirty stories,' said Christopher.

'My liver, alas, will no longer accommodate port,' said Ronnie. 'One of my crosses. A very major one.'

He leant on Patrick's arm, who guided him slowly through the door towards the drawing-room.

Christopher surveyed the debris on the table.

'Isn't it awful,' he said. 'I feel like Ahab and covet Ronnie's vineyard.'

'Then you'd better enlist the help of Jezebel,' said Michael.

'How clever you are, Mike,' said Christopher. 'I didn't know your generation ever read that wonderful book. I want to illustrate it more than anything else in the world.'

They followed the others into the hall. Christopher and Nicholas went into the drawing-room. Michael went through the glass door at the end of the hall. He paused as he heard the sound of running water coming from beyond a green baize door. He pushed it open and saw Lily bending over the sink.

'I'll give you a hand,' he said.

'Ronnie wouldn't approve of that,' she said. 'You might break something.'

'Why doesn't he have any servants?' asked Michael.

'He does. But tonight's their night off. He likes them all to go out at once so that everything runs smoothly for the rest of the week.'

Michael picked up a cloth and started to dry the knives and forks.

'Sit by the fire, Patrick,' said Ronnie. 'You, Christopher, bring over the tray and place that small table near me. Nicholas, would you be so kind as to carry over the brandy. Carefully, please. There! Put it on the table. I think that's everything.'

He picked up a glass and warmed it between his hands. He looked at Patrick and smiled.

'You'll observe the absence of a spirit lamp,' he said. 'A senseless and barbaric Victorian innovation. How would you like your blood heat to be callously raised by the sudden application of a searing flame? Nicholas, perhaps you would place another log on the fire. I think the basket to the right contains the cedar wood.'

He gazed round the company. 'Surely someone's absent?'

'One, two, three, four. Lily is five. It must be Michael,' said Patrick.

Nicholas, who had noticed Michael follow Lily out of the hall, said quickly: 'He went to the bathroom, Ronnie.'

'The *bathroom*?' said Patrick. 'What a simply terrifying refinement. You mean the lavatory, my dear.'

'Now, Patrick, if you feel sufficiently refreshed and are quite comfortable, I think we should proceed to the main business of the evening,' said Ronnie. 'Nicholas, I'm sorry to disturb you again. In that cupboard you will find a box of Turkish delight. Would you place it by me on the table?'

'Business?' said Patrick. 'How can you talk of such a thing? Such a pity to ruin our digestions after such a spread.'

'We must discuss *Eleven*, Patrick,' said Christopher. 'That's why I came to dinner.'

'Nicholas, hand Christopher the cigars,' said Ronnie. He knew that a perfectly good cigar would be wasted. But he had to devise some method of keeping Christopher quiet. Christopher was completely uncouth and uncivilized. He had never learnt to control his thoughts. The dinner they had just eaten could not fail to stimulate thought. But its purpose had not been to loosen a flow of uncontrolled inanities.

Christopher stuck the cigar in his mouth. 'Do you think it makes me look like a tycoon, Ronnie?' he asked.

'You'd better remove the band,' said Ronnie.

Christopher took the cigar from his mouth and twirled it between his fingers. 'Do I smell it or listen to it, Ronnie?' He placed it against his nose.

'Cut it, Christopher.'

Christopher took a used match from the ash tray and jabbed it into the end of the cigar.

Ronnie winced.

'I really don't think it matters now what you do to it, Christopher,' he said. 'I should say that you've bled it to death.'

Christopher looked at Nicholas, winked, and struck a match which he held to the end of the cigar. He coughed, and blew out clouds of smoke.

Ronnie carefully selected his own cigar. One after another he placed them to his ear and tapped them, with a look of concentration on his face. When he had found one to his satisfaction, he cut it carefully, and revolved the end gently in the flame of a match. He dropped the match into the ash tray, leant back against a cushion, and slowly drew in the smoke.

'It would be best, Patrick, if I started by recrossing the territory that we have already mapped,' he said. 'Our organization is as follows. I am the leader. The Scott or the Hunt. I think that you'll agree with me, if I may mix my metaphors, that I must be invested with full executive powers not subject to veto by any other member of the party. You, Christopher, have been engaged as my cartographer. I must speak quite frankly and say that much as I admire your work, I am a little dubious as to your suitability for a position of such great responsibility. The creative artist is seldom critical. Your treatment of my cigars fully illustrates my contention. The third member of the triumvirate is of course Patrick, but without, as I have said, any power of veto. We must now carefully consider what Patrick will dislike most of all. Namely, our objectives. I think we would all agree that with the passing of the plutocracy civilization has virtually ceased to exist in this country. At one time there was some faint hope of a revival of Christianity. But even that has now failed us.'

'I'm afraid I can't agree with you there, Ronnie,' said Christopher. 'Christianity hasn't failed us. The truth is that we must go on suffering as long as we refuse to admit that we murdered Christ.'

'I thought the Jews had suffered for that,' said Patrick.

'So they have,' said Christopher. 'But we still go on persecuting them. They only murdered Christ once, but we crucify them over and over again. I know, because though I'm half Jewish myself I have a wicked urge to persecute them. Gentiles must have double the desire that I have.'

Ronnie jabbed the miniature silver fork into the box of Turkish delight, and placed the sweet into his mouth. He speared a second piece, licked it with the tip of his tongue, before finally swallowing it.

'I really don't see that there's any need for you to enlarge on your theory, Christopher,' said Ronnie. 'I should say that the history of the Jews had been most ably dealt with by Josephus. It hasn't the slightest bearing on the matter we are discussing. I suggest we now try and concentrate on what is obviously the most difficult part of our scheme. The business side. I think we all agree that there isn't one of us qualified to take over the quartermastering. I'm therefore proposing to put Lily in control of that department. You've seen for yourselves some small example of her culinary art. I can promise you that she shows an equal aptitude for sums and figures.'

'This is just like playing Happy Families,' said Patrick. 'You and Lily, I and Nicky. And by the way, Ronnie, I forgot to tell you that I thought it would be a great help to you if Michael joined the staff.'

'Michael? Michael who? Michael Brokowski? My dear Patrick, he can't even speak English!'

'No, no. Michael Henry. One of your guests tonight,' said Patrick.

'I'm afraid I can't see what you're trying to get at. You really mustn't waste time side-tracking me,' said Ronnie.

'I think you're being slightly hard, my dear,' said Patrick. 'I'm sure Michael's just the boy to lick the stamps which Lily is going to put on all those letters you're going to write. I do feel that we should be quite sure that we've first established a happy personal basis to the magazine. I don't want anybody left out in the cold feeling unhappy and neurotic. You mustn't be a greedy old monopolist.'

'I was only thinking about the budget,' said Ronnie. 'We mustn't allow it to become inflated and top heavy.'

He had recovered slightly from the shock of being informed that Michael was going to work for *Eleven*. He started to attack the box of Turkish delight with a speed and regularity that fascinated Patrick who had never seen two pounds of sugar disappear so rapidly.

'We mustn't be mean, Ronnie,' said Patrick. 'On the other hand, I don't want to interfere. You must do entirely what you want.'

'I'm certain Michael wouldn't expect to be paid very much,' said Christopher. 'Certainly not more than Lily.'

'The whole question of salaries will require the most careful thought,' said Ronnie. He omitted to say that he intended to pay

Lily a considerable salary in her capacity as business manager. He was looking forward to the day when she would be in a position to contribute generously to the cost of running the house.

'What about you, Nicky?' said Patrick. 'Would you expect Ronnie to pay you a fat salary?'

'Me, Patrick?' said Nicholas. 'I'd be quite happy to be paid by results.'

Patrick started to laugh. 'So you shall be, my dear. Paid by results! Ronnie's not as kind as some people we know. Perhaps you'd be wiser to get a signed contract out of him.'

'I think we should have Lily here to take a note of what has been said,' announced Ronnie. 'Nicholas, would you be kind enough to find her. She should be in the pantry.'

'If you see Mikey,' said Christopher, 'tell him I've good news for him. If he's not feeling well say that I'm quite ready to go home now.'

As he made his way through the hall Nicholas wondered anxiously what kind of trouble Michael was trying to make. Lily was utterly under Ronnie's thumb. Surely Michael didn't imagine that he could get off with her?

Nicholas reached the door of the pantry, and paused. Beyond the door he heard the sound of Lily laughing. He pushed it open and walked in.

Lily looked startled. She put both hands to her head and started to tidy her hair.

'Ronnie wants you, Lily,' said Nicholas.

She hurried past him and ran down the corridor.

Nicholas looked at Michael. 'Everyone wondered what the devil had happened to you. Even if you were bored it was terribly rude to slide off like that.'

'Who said I was bored?'

'I don't know what you're up to, Michael. But for my sake please be careful.'

'Careful? Careful about what? Are you afraid I may tip over the apple cart?'

Nicholas shrugged his shoulders. 'It doesn't matter. Come on. Let's go and join the others.'

Patrick noticed that Michael was looking extremely pleased with himself as he came into the drawing-room. He looked next at Lily, who appeared flushed and slightly nervous. Christopher had been speaking the truth when he had told him that he wasn't at all happy at Michael having met Lily at his studio. Michael hadn't taken long to assert his hearty charms.

Patrick had no love for Michael. It was clear to him that Michael would go to any lengths to get Nicholas out of what he quite likely referred to as his clutches. But the idea of Michael stealing Lily away from Ronnie was terribly exciting. Ronnie would be so upset. It would be an exquisitely amusing situation.

'Isn't it wonderful, Mikey? Patrick, I mean Ronnie, has agreed that you can work for *Eleven*,' said Christopher.

Michael bowed towards Patrick. 'I trust I shall give complete satisfaction, sir.'

'All this horrid talk of business and money has exhausted me,' said Patrick. 'It's high time I crawled into my little bed.'

'We haven't *started* to talk yet,' said Ronnie.

'Then you'll have to continue without me, my dear. I promise you I'm not missing a second of my beauty sleep.'

Ronnie knew that it was useless to argue with Patrick. 'In that case could you come round here tomorrow morning? We could lunch together. There's a new restaurant in Greek Street. Rumour has reached me that they can offer a very fair bouillabaisse. I'm told that it even contains the essential *rascasse*.'

'I'm going to Paris tomorrow,' said Patrick.

'What!' exclaimed Nicholas. 'You never told me.'

'Didn't I? Should I have done? Or am I just being particularly dense tonight?'

'How wonderful to be able to go where you like just like that,' said Christopher. 'You must do lots of propaganda for *Eleven* while you're there, Patrick. I know all your smart friends will subscribe to it, if you ask them to.'

Ronnie was on the point of suggesting that it would be a very good idea if he went with Patrick to Paris. On the other hand, it would be quite useful to have him out of the way for a few days. It would give him a chance to establish *Eleven* without interference from Patrick. It would leave him a clear field. Not quite. There was still Nicholas. Patrick had said something about wanting Nicholas to work for *Eleven* so that he could keep an eye on his interests. It would be even better if Nicholas could be got out of the way too.

'Perhaps it wouldn't be a bad idea if you took Nicholas along with you, Patrick,' he said. 'I can give him introductions to the fashion houses in Paris. He can go round and establish contact with them in the capacity of a public relations officer.'

'That *is* difficult of you, Ronnie. I've only reserved one seat on the plane,' said Patrick.

'I don't want to go to Paris,' said Nicholas.

'That's nothing to do with it. You must do exactly as Ronnie tells you,' said Patrick.

'Couldn't I come with you, Patrick?' said Christopher. 'I'm terribly good at missions. Especially cultural ones.'

Patrick started to move towards the door. Nicholas hesitated. If Patrick wanted to go to bed he could. But he was staying with the others.

Ronnie got up from the sofa. 'If Patrick's going, I'm afraid our meeting must come to an end,' he said. He started to shepherd his guests towards the door.

When they reached the front door, Patrick said: 'It all went splendidly, Ronnie. I think *Eleven's* going to be a very happy magazine.'

Ronnie closed the front door.

'You can lock up now, Lily,' he said. 'I shall go and work in the study. You needn't wait up for me. Breakfast about eleven, I think.'

Nicholas sat as far away as possible from Patrick in the corner of the Rolls. Now and again he glanced towards him and studied his face in the lights of the oncoming traffic. Patrick did not look once in his direction.

Nicholas was surprised when the car suddenly stopped.

'We get out here,' said Patrick.

Nicholas looked out of the window.

'You're lost, Nicky,' said Patrick. 'You're far too cross to know where you are.'

'I'm not cross. Just surprised. Why didn't you tell me before that you were going away tomorrow? Anyway, where are we?'

'There you are. You are lost! Don't you recognize *la trappe*? Are you coming up? Or would you be happier here?'

Nicholas got out of the car. He supposed that Patrick had called at his flat to collect something that he'd forgotten, before going back to the Rialto.

The first thing Nicholas noticed as they walked into the flat was his suitcase in the hall.

'What on earth . . . ?' he began.

'Didn't I tell you? I've had all your clothes moved round here. I do hope you won't mind. I didn't feel the Rialto was a great success. It didn't seem to agree with you. Of course, if I'm wrong you must go back there this minute. But it was rather large, wasn't it? And perhaps just a little vulgar?'

'What am I going to do tomorrow if you're going away? Do you want me to stay here?'

'I think perhaps you'd better come with me after all. It'll be too horrid for you here all on your own.'

'I don't want to come,' said Nicholas. 'In any case I can't.' He was very angry. Patrick was treating him like a piece of furniture that could be shoved backwards or forwards as he pleased.

'Can't? Can't?' said Patrick. 'That's a word I was taught never to use.'

Nicholas did not reply. He walked past Patrick into the sitting-room. He stared in utter amazement at the iron bedstead which had been set up in the centre of the room. Behind him he heard Patrick begin to laugh.

'I'm afraid it's not very smart, my dear,' said Patrick. 'It was the best I could do at the time of night. The porter and I had a terrible job getting it through the door. All the time I was picturing Ronnie getting more and more upset as his dinner began to spoil.'

'So that's what you were doing!' said Nicholas. 'I can't see that it was necessary. I could have managed perfectly well for one night.'

'You've no idea how hard my floors are,' said Patrick. He closed the door.

Nicholas was alone in the sitting-room. He went and sat down on the bed. The springs creaked beneath his weight. He knew that the evening had been a disaster. He had thoroughly upset Patrick. Everything had gone wrong. Everything had been against him. Patrick hadn't yet forgiven him for the rebuff before they had gone out to dinner. He had probably been infuriated further over the incident of the cheque, because he hadn't come running back asking him to sign it. Patrick was under the impression that he had bought him lock, stock and barrel. But he wasn't a slave.

Nicholas was under no illusion as to the significance of the sudden move from the Rialto. The iron bedstead had not been substituted for the double-sprung mattress for nothing. It was a reminder that he was not coming up to expectations.

Nicholas stood up and lit a cigarette. He couldn't deny it. He had taken too much and given nothing in return. By accepting what Patrick gave him he entered into a contract. There was nothing legally binding about it, but the terms were implied. It might be an unwritten law. The fact remained that one always had to pay for what one had.

He undressed slowly, put on his dressing gown and walked into the hall. As he was about to knock on the door of Patrick's room, he heard the key turn in the lock.

Patrick was very, very angry.

FIVE

Nicholas felt a finger tickling the lobe of his ear. He opened his eyes and saw Patrick leaning over his bed.

'Goodbye, lazy one,' he said.

Nicholas sat up quickly.

'Patrick, when are you coming back?' he asked.

Patrick put on his gloves. 'I really hadn't thought about it,' he said. 'Three days, three weeks, three months? Who knows?'

'Seriously.'

'Seriously,' Patrick mimicked. 'Why are you so worried, little one?'

'What shall I do while you're away?'

'Whatever you feel like. You can stay here and order whatever you choose.'

'I ought to do some work.'

Patrick was puzzled. 'Work? Ah, of course, your work. You'd better telephone Ronnie and see if he can suggest anything. Now snuggle down under the bedclothes before you catch cold.'

Nicholas obeyed. He prayed that Patrick was about to ask him to go with him to Paris. He was so friendly. He couldn't possibly still be angry.

'I only ask one thing of you,' said Patrick. '*Do* be careful of the pictures. If you don't like them turn them to the wall. But please don't throw things at them.'

He moved towards the door.

Now, thought Nicholas, he's going to ask me to come with him. He knows that I'm lying here waiting for him to ask me.

Patrick opened the door, turned and waved.

'Au revoir, Nicky,' he said. 'I'm sorry you decided last night not to come with me.'

'But Patrick . . .'

The door closed.

Nicholas hurled back the bedclothes and leapt out of bed. He threw his dressing gown round his shoulders. There was only one bedroom slipper by his bed. By the time he had found the other it was too late. He heard the lift doors clang outside in the corridor.

He sat down on the edge of the bed and stared through the windows at the trees in the park. He heard the rattle of milk bottles in the distance. A car hooted in the street. He looked at his watch. Seven-thirty. He lay down on the bed listening to the noises of the city as it started to go to work. Millions of people would soon be fighting their way on to buses and into tubes or hurrying along on foot. Soon they would be pouring into offices, factories and shops.

Nicholas lay on his bed. He had nothing to do. There was no need for him to get up. He was superannuated at twenty-one.

As he lay there he knew that he had missed his chance to start work on the *Gladiator*. He had known it from the moment Patrick met him at the station. He had now spent three days with Patrick. Each day had seen his resistance grow weaker. In three days Patrick had completely obliterated his independence.

Patrick had won an easy battle. He had known from the beginning that Nicholas was frightened of the *Gladiator*. It hadn't needed much effort to persuade him that there were more agreeable occupations. The offer of a job on *Eleven* had supplied Nicholas with the excuse that he was looking for. It had been a sop to his conscience. The next step was simple. Patrick had only to abandon *Eleven*, and Nicholas would be delivered entirely into his hands.

Nicholas was unable to go back to sleep. He put out his hand and pressed the bell.

A few minutes later he heard the sound of a key being turned in the lock. The valet came into the room.

'I'd like some breakfast, please,' said Nicholas.

'Sorry. Quite out of the question,' said the valet.

'I don't understand. I was told to order what I wanted.'

'That may be. You can have a drink if you like. We don't cater here. If you want food you have to order it the day before. There was only one breakfast ordered here for this morning. Will you be moving out today?'

'Of course not,' said Nicholas.

He hated the man for his insinuations. He hadn't even troubled to be polite. Any moment he expected him to say: 'Come off it. Stop giving yourself airs. I know all about you. You're just another one-night stand. At least my job's steadier than yours.'

The valet closed the door.

Nicholas looked round the room. He was filled with a sudden loathing for the flat. All he wanted to do was to get out of it as quickly as possible. He dressed hurriedly and took the lift down.

As he was passing through the foyer the hall porter accosted him. 'Leave your key behind.'

'I'm staying,' said Nicholas.

'Quite. But it would be safer with me. We've lost so many already.' He held out his hand. Nicholas gave him the key.

It wasn't until Nicholas had gone out of the building that he realized the full implication of the porter's remark. Patrick was continually losing his keys because a succession of young men were always walking off with them. Nicholas was so angry that he nearly went back to ask the porter what exactly he had meant. He had no right to sneer at him as just another of Patrick's pick-ups.

Nicholas kept walking. He was in an impossible position. He was too vulnerable. Anyone could insult him as much as they liked. He couldn't answer back.

Nicholas walked along Piccadilly. He was passing under the arches of the Ritz when he decided that the time had come to extract himself from his compromising position. He realized that he was getting out of his depth. The situation was becoming dangerous. Soon it would be too late. If he was going to get away from Patrick, he would have to act now. He must have nothing more to do with Patrick if he wanted to retain a vestige of his own personality.

Nicholas had no objections to spending Patrick's money. He was prepared to use anyone who could help him. He would go so far as to say that he had no moral objection to being kept by Patrick. Unfortunately Patrick expected too much. Patrick wanted to possess him entirely. He would never allow him any life of his own. Certainly not any success of his own. All his actions and achieve-

ments would have to be Patrick's doing. Patrick had to organize
and rule his existence. He wanted in fact to eat him alive.

By the time Nicholas reached Fortnum & Mason his determi-
nation to leave Patrick began to waver. It was always unwise to
do anything in a rush on the spur of the moment. There was no
point in upsetting Patrick needlessly. If he was careful it might be
possible to establish a relationship with Patrick on a different basis.
After all, Patrick could be very useful to him.

Nicholas felt hungry. He crossed Piccadilly Circus and made his
way along Coventry Street to Lyons Corner House.

When he had paid for his breakfast he had thirty shillings left.
Patrick would be away for at least three days. The immediate
problem was to borrow sufficient money to keep him solvent until
Patrick returned. There weren't many sources that he could tap.
Michael and possibly Christopher. He made his way on foot in
the direction of the Fulham Road. At each step he regretted more
and more that he had not agreed to go with Patrick to Paris when
he had been asked the night before. He should have swallowed
his pride more quickly. He had been right to refuse the first time,
but not the second. It was something to remember in future. One
should make a brief display of protestation quickly followed by a
graceful acceptance. If one wasn't careful one found oneself not
even in the position of being able to refuse.

Nicholas realized that the hurried removal from the Rialto the
night before had been contrived with a purpose. So had Patrick's
sudden departure for Paris. Both were warnings that he mustn't
think for one moment that he was indispensable.

By the time he had walked to Christopher's studio, he felt hot
and exhausted. He pressed the bell and leant against the railings.
The window above his head opened and Michael called out: 'God!
Jehu without his chariot. What have you done with the Rolls?
Flogged it? Wait a second. I'll come down and let you in.'

Nicholas followed Michael up the stairs into the studio.

'Where's Christopher?' he asked.

'He'll be back in a moment. He felt neurotic and went for a
walk. What's happened to Daddy this morning?'

'He's flown to Paris.'

'Alone?'

'I suppose so.'

'You only suppose so. Aren't you sure? Then who was the friend he took with him?'

'Friend? I'm sure that's not true.'

Michael started to laugh. 'My God, you are jumpy. Still, I don't blame you seeing all that lovely lolly slip away. Don't worry. I don't know and I don't care who went with him.'

'It's all very well for you,' said Nicholas.

'Of course it is. For Christ's sake don't lose your sense of humour, Nicky.'

Nicholas smiled. 'You shouldn't mock me. It isn't much fun being Tantalus. Every time I stretch out my hand the river of gold recedes. It's disheartening.'

'That's the way to talk!' said Michael. 'I feel a lot better now. I'll make a success of you yet. The trouble with you is you're too bloody soft and sentimental. Put yourself in my hands and I'll change all that, I promise you. The first thing I've got to do is to bring up a few blisters on your heart and toughen up those flabby bowels.'

'Why?'

'Because I want to turn you into an impersonal piece of machinery. There's only one way of getting the honey, and that's by becoming an extractor.'

'What on earth's that?'

'Don't tell me you've never seen one. I thought you'd had the benefits of a rustic upbringing. It's a cunning machine for removing the honey from the cells where the bees store it. You place the honey sections in the extractor and turn the handle. The sections whirl round and round and out flies the honey. The faster you turn the handle the faster the honey flows. Simple, isn't it? Now all you've got to do is to start leading Patrick a merry old dance. The faster . . .'

'Are you as unscrupulous as you like to pretend?' said Nicholas.

Michael started to pace up and down the studio.

'Yes, I really am,' he said. 'Why not? Where does morality get you? Nowhere, because there's no such thing as morality. It's a lot of bloody eye-wash thought up by humbugging materialists who want to keep what they've got. We're living in a material world whatever anyone may try to tell you to the contrary. The world is ruled by only one principle. Selfishness. Until you grasp that you're nothing but a lamb in a den of thieving lions. You haven't a hope of surviving with your silly woolliness against their claws.'

'Don't burst a blood vessel,' said Nicholas.

'Don't you realize that we're living in crazyland? If you show affection for anybody, all they do is despise you. But kick them about and it's a different story. They'll come running after you because they respect you.'

'I don't see what this has to do with me,' said Nicholas.

'Why the hell do you think Patrick went off without you. Because you weren't affectionate enough? Balls! Treat him like dirt. Pop him into the extractor. Then you'll find he thinks you're someone worth troubling about.'

'This is just some ridiculous theory you've thought up overnight.'

'Do you think so? Look at Christopher. He thinks I'm wonderful. There's nothing he won't do for me. I'm young Britain lost in the fog. Why do you think he wants to help me? Because I treat him like dirt. If I kick him with one boot he goes down on his knees and begs me to kick him with the other.'

'Oh, rubbish!'

'Look at Ronnie. How does he treat Lily? He rubs her nose in the dirt and she dotes on him.'

'Is that how you treated her last night?'

Michael laughed. 'Never you mind! What do you think of her? Isn't she marvellous? To look at, I mean.'

'Yes.'

'Christopher doesn't think so. But Lily's the girl for me!'

'God, what vanity!' said Nicholas. 'You're talking as if she couldn't wait for you.'

'She can't. I'm going to need some help from you. But not a word to Christopher. He's not to be trusted. He can't help blurting out the truth.'

'You'd better leave Lily alone. You can't do a thing like that to Ronnie.'

'Can't I?'

'You can count me out. I'll have nothing to do with it.'

'Don't be such a bloody idiot. No one will find out. If they do, I don't care.'

'I do. What's the matter with you this morning? Have you started to go out of your mind?'

'I'll tell you what's the matter with me,' said Michael slowly. 'I'll tell you my darkest secret. Would you really like to know what makes me behave like this? Why I love stamping on Christopher? Why I'm longing to spit in Ronnie's face? Why I'd love to see you make a beggar of Patrick?'

He drew the automatic out of his hip pocket and laid it in the palm of his hand.

'Because I'm *bored*,' he shouted. 'Bored to death by everyone's lies and hypocrisy.'

Nicholas looked at the gun and saw that Michael's hand was shaking.

'You really are going out of your mind,' he said. 'The trouble with you is that your nerves are unemployed. You'd better find something for them to feed on pretty quickly.'

'Don't worry. I'm clearing out soon. After I've settled a few scores.'

'So you're just going to cause as much trouble as possible because nobody's taken any notice of you,' said Nicholas. 'The best thing you can do is to pick up that telephone and ring the *Gladiator* and tell Andrews you want to start flying for him. I suppose you think Patrick had some hidden motive in fixing that up for you?'

'Do you mean to say you don't know?'

Nicholas shook his head.

'Christ, what a bloody innocent! I'll fly all right. But when I'm ready. I'll explain it . . .'

He stopped talking as he heard the downstairs door open and the sound of footsteps coming up the stairs.

Nicholas said quickly: 'Can you lend me some money?'

'I'm flat broke. You'd better ask Christopher. No. Leave him to me.'

'Open the door please, Mike,' called Christopher.

Michael sauntered to the door and kicked it open.

Christopher stood in the doorway grinning at them through an armful of roses.

'A bloody flower girl!' said Michael.

'Hullo, Nicky,' said Christopher. 'Aren't they beautiful? I bought them for you, Mike.' He dropped the roses on to a chair. 'Have we any iodine? I've pricked my thumb.'

'Suck it,' said Michael.

'Isn't he brutal?' said Christopher. 'I believe he'd watch me bleed to death without moving. How's Patrick, Nicky? I think it's terribly unkind of him not to take you to Paris with him. When people are fond of one another, and I'm sure he's very fond of you, I can't understand why they must go deliberately out of their way to torture one another.'

'How clearly you express yourself,' said Michael.

'Oh dear. I've made you angry again,' said Christopher. 'It's not my fault if I can't help saying exactly what I feel. It's my natural impetuosity. For instance, when I saw those roses just now I couldn't stop myself buying the whole lot at enormous expense. I suppose it was because they reminded me of my childhood. You see, my grandmother, the one on the Jewish side of my family, used to grow . . .'

'Nicky would hate to hear about your grandmother's roses,' said Michael. 'He wants to borrow some money.'

Christopher giggled. 'I was about to ask him to lend me some. I've just spent every penny I had on me.'

'Then you'd better get to the bank before it closes,' said Michael.

'I'll go this minute. Would you like to come with us, Nicky? It's a wonderful day out.'

'I'll stay here and smell the roses,' said Michael. 'I'll ring you later, Nicky, if I don't see you first.'

As Christopher and Nicholas stepped into the street, Christopher said: 'I'm awfully worried about Michael. He's so terribly mixed up. He makes me feel as if I'm deliberately keeping him in a cage. I'm afraid when the portrait's finished he'll fly away. Poor Mikey. There's nothing I can do for him. He makes me feel impotent. All the bravado in the world can't conceal the tragedy of his lost soul. What do you think will become of him, Nicky? You're an old friend of his. Can't you do something for him?'

'I may have been a friend once,' said Nicholas. 'But friendship isn't something that keeps on its own. It's rather like a fire. You have to keep putting fuel on it or else it goes out. Between Michael and me there's nothing but a heap of cold ashes. We forgot to make the fire up.'

'But that's horrible,' said Christopher. 'You must . . .'

'Here's the bank,' said Nicholas.

'So it is. Come in. I do hope they'll cash a cheque for me. The manager doesn't seem to be able to grasp that I can't keep track of my account.'

'Don't worry. I've got enough to go on with,' said Nicholas.

'But Nicky . . .'

'I've got enough, Christopher. Thanks all the same.'

Nicholas left Christopher on the steps of the bank and walked away.

When he reached the corner of the street he wasn't quite sure why he hadn't wanted to borrow money from Christopher. If he could take it from Patrick he should be able to take it from anyone. The truth was that he would never make a very good extractor.

He made his way on foot in the direction of Ronnie Gras' house.

Ronnie sat up in bed and smiled with anticipation when he saw the bunch of grapes that Lily had placed on the table by his bed.

'You can draw the curtains. Just a little,' he said.

He raised the cluster of muscats to his nostrils, inhaled their bouquet, and started to tear them with his teeth from the bunch.

'Lily, dear. Would you hold them for me? I find it so tiring to the arm.'

He made himself comfortable against the pillows, stretched out his legs, and opened his mouth. Lily held the bunch in front of his mouth. He continued to nibble at the rich juicy fruit.

'Exquisite!' he murmured.

Lily leant over him and wiped his face with a clean napkin.

'They were a present from Patrick, dear. He also sent a basket of peaches,' she said.

'How extraordinary. Those grapes were really quite delicious. Patrick usually has such atrocious taste. You know, Lily, Patrick is a philistine. Beneath that shining veneer, there's an abysmal amount of ignorance and stupidity. Some people fall into the error of thinking he's cultured. But all his thoughts are secondhand. He culls them from the glossy magazines.'

He turned over, propped himself on his elbow and looked at Lily. 'That's why I decline to be a member of his sycophantic circle. I can only talk about him this way in the morning. It's the one time of the day when I can be honest with myself. I'm perfectly aware that later on I become too worldly.'

Lily sat on the bed, leant over and kissed him on the forehead.

'Not there, please,' he said. 'I hate being kissed where my hair is receding. I'm reminded of my age. Your lips are turned to icicles.'

'Shall I kiss you on your favourite place?'

The door bell started to ring.

'Bother!' he said. 'Never mind. It's probably the post. If there're any exciting parcels bring them up and I'll open them in bed.'

Lily went down and opened the front door.

'Good morning,' said Nicholas. 'I'm sorry to trouble you. Could I see Ronnie?'

'I don't know. You'd better come in. He's just finished breakfast. He'll be down soon. You won't mind waiting, will you?'

'Not at all. Thank you very much again for dinner last night.'

'I'm so glad you enjoyed it. You'd better wait in the morning room. You'll find the papers there and there are cigarettes in the box.'

Ronnie started calling from upstairs.

His face fell as she came into the bedroom empty-handed.

'It's Nicholas Milestone. He wants to see you,' she said.

'Oh that inefficient Post Office!' he grumbled. 'Always late. What does he want? Doesn't he know I never see anyone here without an appointment? Send him away.'

Lily moved towards the door.

'Not yet. Not yet. I want my bath run. And you'd better lay out my fawn suit. There's a little sunshine this morning, I think.'

Nicholas wandered about the morning room looking absent-mindedly at the pictures. He was not quite sure why he had decided to come and see Ronnie. It sounded rather silly to say to Ronnie that he wanted something to do. Ronnie was obviously the last person to approve of work of any kind.

As Lily was half way down the stairs on her way to tell Nicholas that Ronnie could not see him, the door bell rang again. At the bottom of the stairs she hesitated, then crossed the hall and opened the front door.

There was no one outside. A taxi was disappearing round the curve of the crescent.

On the steps lay a bunch of roses. She stooped, gathered them up and carried them into the house.

Ronnie called: 'Is that the parcel post at last? Bring them up. I'm in the bathroom.'

Lily went upstairs and carried the flowers into the bathroom.

'Who on earth could have sent me roses?' exclaimed Ronnie.

'I don't know.'

'Read the card.'

'I don't understand it.'

'In that case they're sure to be from Patrick,' said Ronnie. 'What does the card say?'

'*Veni, vidi*. Then there's a space with a question mark at the end,' said Lily.

'I don't understand it at all. To what can we attribute this sudden flowering of the classics?'

'I couldn't say, dear.' She laid the flowers on the bathroom chair. 'Do you want me to scrub your back today?'

'Yes, yes. But not too hard. Just a gentle stimulation of the circulation with the finger tips. What charming roses! I wonder what they are? Hybrids, of course.'

'Do you want to play with your boats today?' asked Lily.

'Of course. But you're not to refer to my tummy as a sand-bank.'

He lay back in the soothing hot water. Lily took a gaily painted clockwork launch from the cupboard and wound it up. She handed it to Ronnie, who adjusted the rudder and let it go in his bath. He lay entranced as he watched the craft nose its way along the sides of the bath. When it got into difficulties with a brush or piece of soap, he helped it on with a flick of his toes. When it looked like going too fast he splashed up the water with his hands, and chuckled as it plunged its bow into the heavy seas.

Downstairs Nicholas was growing impatient. Several times he opened the door and looked out into the deserted hall. As the minutes ticked by he became more and more convinced that Ronnie was deliberately keeping him cooling his heels.

Nicholas had been waiting an hour when Lily came down the stairs, and carried the roses into the morning room.

'I'm so sorry to have kept you waiting,' she said. 'I'm afraid Ronnie wanted me.'

Nicholas stared at the roses.

'Aren't they beautiful?' she said. 'Ronnie thinks Patrick sent them to him.'

'Patrick? To Ronnie?' exclaimed Nicholas.

'Is anything the matter? Don't you like them?'

Nicholas went to the table where the roses were lying and cupped one of the blooms between his hands. 'They're a most unusual colour,' he said.

'I've never seen any like them before,' she said. 'I'm terribly sorry, but Ronnie says he hasn't got time to see you this morning.'

'I must see him.'

'Perhaps you'd better telephone him later. He said he's sure you'll understand.'

She walked towards the door. Nicholas followed her across the hall. She held open the front door for him. 'I'm so sorry Ronnie can't see you,' she said.

'So am I. . . . I can't get over those roses. It's an extraordinary thing but I saw some just like them at Christopher's studio an hour ago.'

'Really?' she said. 'I suppose they must be fashionable now.'

As Nicholas walked down the steps he was so interested in the roses that he forgot to be angry with Ronnie. If they were the same ones he had seen at the studio, what were they doing at Ronnie's house? Christopher wouldn't have brought them. It must have been Michael. There was only one person he would have brought them for. Lily.

Nicholas strolled slowly along the crescent.

'Slung out on your neck?'

Nicholas stopped. 'Michael! So it was you! They were Christopher's roses!'

'You mean the roses Christopher gave me.'

'What's he going to say when he finds you've walked off with them?'

'It's not what he's going to say. It's what he said. Their beauty was already beginning to make him feel guilty. He felt that it was wrong for him to enjoy them when some sick person in hospital might be cheered by them. Never mind him. What was Lily's reaction?'

'She thought they'd been sent to Ronnie.'

'Don't you believe it.'

'It's the truth. She worships Ronnie. He can't do anything wrong in her eyes. She dotes on him.'

'God, you're green!' said Michael. 'No wonder you can't handle Patrick. I tell you she doesn't care tuppence for Ronnie. She's just grown accustomed to him. He's become a bad habit. But he's kept her in the cage far too long. No woman can tolerate that for ever. Lily's fed up with living in isolation. She's longing to escape and spread her wings. I tell you she's ripe for the plucking. My frontal attack has swept her off her feet. She's tasting the heaven of being hunted again. She's quivering with excitement at the thought of me!'

'You've got a chance!' said Nicholas.

'I bet you anything you like I'll have her before the day's out,' said Michael.

'Sheer fantasy!'

'I suppose you won't believe me when I tell you I've already arranged an assignation with her at Patrick's flat at six this evening.'

'Oh no you don't,' said Nicholas. 'I don't want anything to do with this squalid affair. I'm in enough trouble already.'

'There's nothing for you to worry about. All that's happening is that Lily will be going out for a couple of hours this evening. I've got to meet her somewhere, haven't I? I can't take her to the studio in case Christopher's there. I can't afford an hotel. Patrick's flat is the obvious answer. But you'll have to let me in. I'm not on friendly terms with the hall porter like you. That's all I'm asking you to do. What's the objection? Surely not sympathy for that slug Ronnie? I bet he's just ignored you and slung you out.'

'As a matter of fact . . .'

'I knew it. He treats you like dirt. Don't fool yourself. He only tolerates you when Patrick's about. The moment he's out of the way Ronnie doesn't attempt to conceal his contempt for you. Besides, what harm will it do him? He'll never know.'

Nicholas hesitated. 'All right,' he said. 'I'll let you into Patrick's flat. I'll be waiting for you there at six.'

'That's the way to talk. You'd better come and lunch with me and Christopher,' said Michael. 'This calls for a celebration.'

Nicholas looked at Michael. He expected to see some signs of madness in his eyes. But all he saw was the round handsome face laughing at him.

'I'm not hungry,' he said. 'I feel like exercise. I think I'll walk for a bit.'

'See you at six then,' said Michael. He stopped a taxi, got in, and drove away.

Nicholas walked along the pavement and turned through the wrought iron gates that led into the park. As he strolled across the grass his resentment against Ronnie increased. Michael had been quite right. The moment Patrick was out of the way Ronnie had made no attempt to conceal his contempt.

Nicholas sat down on a bench. The thought of Michael making a fool of Ronnie gave him a sense of pleasure.

All the same he was slightly worried.

As the hands of the Regency clock on the mantelpiece approached six o'clock, Nicholas began to feel uneasy. He began to hope that Michael would not turn up. He no longer felt such a willing fellow-conspirator. He thought of the maxim that if one played with fire one got one's fingers burned.

At ten past six he began to feel happier. It was clear that Michael wasn't coming after all. It had been sheer fabrication on his part.

Nicholas put on his coat. He had given Michael ten minutes. If Michael turned up now it was too late. He would have only himself to blame.

As Nicholas opened the door he heard the lift stop. Michael pulled back the gates and stepped out.

'What the devil . . . ?'

'I was just going. I thought you weren't coming.'

'Aren't you going to offer me a drink first?'

'I'm late as it is.'

'Don't come back before nine,' said Michael.

Nicholas hesitated. He was on the point of calling the whole thing off. Michael wouldn't be pleased. But he was playing with fire.

'Look, Michael . . .' he began.

Michael pushed past him into the flat. 'Have a good time, Nicky,' he said. 'I know I'm going to.'

He closed the door behind him.

Nicholas was angry with himself as he stepped out into the street. He was incapable of making any decisions. He did what people told him to do. As a result he had landed himself with three hours to kill. He would much rather have stayed quietly in Patrick's flat. He thought vaguely of going to a pub to have a drink. But he hadn't much money. If he had stayed in the flat he could have ordered drinks on Patrick's account. There was only one thing to do. Go to a cinema.

He walked to Leicester Square, bought a ticket, and went into the Odeon.

To begin with he was unable to concentrate on the film. He kept thinking about what was taking place in the flat. But gradually the soporific effect of the picture calmed him. It seemed that whatever might be happening in Patrick's flat had nothing to do with him. It was like something that was taking place in another world.

It was five minutes to nine when he came out of the cinema. He felt almost light-hearted as he made his way through the jostling crowds along Piccadilly. The three hours had not been nearly as painful and worrying as he had feared.

When the hall porter told him that the key was still upstairs, Nicholas hesitated. He was about to return to the street when he changed his mind. Michael had promised to be out of the flat by nine. It was now quarter past. He had done more than enough for Michael for one day. The probability was that he was upstairs in the flat alone, helping himself to Patrick's drink.

He came out of the lift, walked along the passage, and pressed the bell.

He heard the sitting-room door inside the flat open and some-one come into the hall.

Patrick opened the door.

Nicholas stared at him with his mouth open. The blood raced to his face.

'Aren't you coming in?' said Patrick.

'But you're in Paris.'

'Am I? I don't think so.'

Nicholas walked past him into the sitting-room. He looked quickly round. There was no one in the flat except Patrick.

'What's the matter, funny one? You look out of breath. Have you walked up the stairs? Don't say the lift has broken down again. I couldn't bear it.'

'When did you get back?'

'Ten, twelve minutes ago. Have you had a lovely day, my dear?'

'I thought you would be away for at least three days.'

'You don't sound at all pleased to see me. I'm awfully sorry if you didn't want me to come back. I'd better go away again.'

'It's wonderful to see you,' Nicholas managed to say. 'But what happened?'

'Would you believe it. It was actually raining in Paris. Have you ever heard of such a thing? Rain in Paris but sun in London.'

Nicholas calculated that if Patrick had only been back ten min-utes the odds were that he had not seen Michael. He might of course be playing cat and mouse, waiting to see how he would give himself away.

'How serious you look,' said Patrick. 'Yes. I can see that I shall have to go.'

'I'm sorry, Patrick. I'm feeling rather tired.'

'Sorry? But you mustn't feel sorry when there's nothing to be sorry about.' He ran his fingers through Nicholas's hair.

Nicholas said: 'What's happened to this room? It's grown larger. Oh, of course. The iron bed's been taken out.'

'It was too hideous. I can't think why I ever had it brought here,' said Patrick.

Nicholas felt sure that Patrick knew nothing. He had come back because he could not stay away from him. Patrick was crazy about him, however much he pretended not to be.

Nicholas got up from the arm of the chair where he had been sitting, sat down next to Patrick on the sofa and put his arm round him.

'He-man!' said Patrick laughing. 'Now tell me all your news. What have you been up to today? No. Don't move. I feel so invigorated with that great strong arm round me. Whom did you see today?'

'Christopher and Michael.'

'Not Ronnie?'

'He wouldn't see me. He doesn't like me.'

'We'll have to alter that, won't we? I'm afraid he only really likes himself. That's what fascinates me about him. He's not very pretty but he seems to find himself madly attractive.'

'I don't see that gives him the right to be downright insulting to me.'

'There, there. Don't worry, my dear. We'll put him in his place, shall we? If he's been nasty to you, he'll have to be punished. I promise you I won't allow him to get away with that kind of behaviour. How was Christopher? Was he kind to you?'

'I only saw him for a few minutes. Michael was bullying him as usual.'

'What a strange boy Michael is. He's rather like Ronnie in some ways. Far better looking though.'

Nicholas began to relax. He had had a narrow escape but it was quite clear that Patrick knew nothing about Michael. Perhaps

Michael hadn't even made use of the flat. The whole thing might well have been pure fantasy.

'Shall we go out tonight, Patrick?' he asked. 'Just the two of us. I've had an awfully boring day. I feel like celebrating your return. Look. You go and change. I'll put on my best suit and new bow tie.'

'Rather gay for someone so tired, aren't we?'

'You've made me forget it.'

Patrick smiled at Nicholas, disengaged himself, and went into his bedroom.

Nicholas went into the kitchen, took some ice from the refrigerator, came back and mixed a martini.

He was feeling very pleased with himself. He had handled Patrick beautifully. He had shown just the right amount of affection. His fortunes had been at their lowest ebb that morning. In a few minutes they had soared to the heights.

'Nicholas,' called Patrick.

Nicholas sauntered into the bedroom.

Patrick was sitting on the edge of his bed looking at the *New Yorker*. Without looking up he said: 'Besides being a filthy habit to smoke in the bedroom as I've already told you, I can't say I admire the colour of your lipstick.'

He held out his hand and pointed to the ash tray on the bedside table.

From where he was standing Nicholas could see the stubs smeared with red.

'But Patrick . . .' he began.

'My dear, you've turned the colour of a lobster. I'm so glad you've had such a successful day. Our country cousins don't waste much time, do they? Rather a case of the cat being away, wasn't it? I do think you might have shown a little more intelligence and cleared up the remains of your sordid frolic. You must know that I'm old enough to appreciate that the young can't help being unfaithful. But I did think you were clever enough to understand that we old things like to pretend that it isn't true. We do object to having it rubbed in our faces. Of course I don't know much about you *normals*. You may arrange things differently in your world. I wouldn't know.'

He continued to turn over the pages of the magazine.

Nicholas looked at the ash tray and back again at Patrick.

'Don't stand there gawking as if it's all my fault,' said Patrick angrily. 'Take it away. Then perhaps you'd telephone the Rialto and reserve me a room. Afterwards no doubt you'll arrange to have this entire flat fumigated.'

The tone of his voice warned Nicholas that now was not the moment to attempt an explanation. He picked up the ash tray, carried it into the sitting-room, and emptied it into the waste paper basket. There was not much time to think out a convincing explanation. His future was suspended precariously in the balance. It wasn't the time to think of loyalties. He had only himself to consider. After such unforgivable carelessness Michael wasn't entitled to any protection.

He returned to the bedroom carrying the ash tray.

'Take that thing out of here at once,' said Patrick. 'You should have remembered that I never smoke in my bedroom.'

'Nor do I,' said Nicholas. He spoke angrily. Patrick looked directly at him for the first time. Seizing his advantage Nicholas added: 'What do you take me for? A complete idiot?'

'My dear, you're shouting.'

'I should be bloody well crying! Now I know just how much you trust me.'

'Whenever did I say I trusted you?'

'I was a fool to imagine you did. I'll ring the Rialto.'

While he was speaking to the receptionist at the Rialto Nicholas knew that he had intrigued Patrick with his outburst. Patrick was mystified. He wasn't the sort of person who could ignore a mystery without trying to unravel it.

When he had replaced the telephone, he picked up his drink, and sat down under the window.

Patrick came in from the bedroom still holding the *New Yorker*. He looked at the glass in Nicholas's hand. 'Am I allowed one?' he asked.

Nicholas got up and poured Patrick a drink. 'I've arranged a room for you at the Rialto,' he said gruffly.

'How kind you are.' Patrick sipped his drink. 'Quite delicious. Where did you learn to mix martinis?'

Nicholas knew that Patrick would never ask him a direct question. Patrick was waiting for the explanation without asking for it.

'I suppose you're waiting to hear my excuses,' said Nicholas.

'What a funny thing to say. You make me feel like a schoolmaster.'

'You've just behaved like one. . . . This had nothing to do with me at all. . . . Well, not much . . . But I'm not going to be punished for something I never did.'

'You're not going to *sneak*, I hope.'

'I haven't any alternative. But you mustn't mention it to anyone.'

'I'm not very good with secrets, my dear. The only point of them as far as I can see is the exquisite pleasure of sharing them with other people.'

'Michael came here earlier this evening. He told me he was going to meet Lily. Don't ask me how he arranged it. I don't know. I wouldn't have let him use your flat only I was furious with Ronnie for the way he treated me this morning . . .'

Patrick interrupted: 'My dear, don't apologize. But this is fascinating. Absolutely fascinating.'

'You believe me?'

'Of course I do. I know you're sometimes rather difficult. But I never really believed you were so foolish. You're a clever person, Nicky. That's why I like you so much. Besides, it didn't fit in with your character. I never thought of you as a Beastly Man. . . . What did Lily think she was playing at? The naughty girl!'

He placed his glass on the table and sat down beside Nicholas on the sofa.

'Funny one, you've made my day quite perfect,' he said. 'A moment ago it looked as if you'd ruined it. I'm sorry I'm such a jealous old thing. But you're so delicious I want to gobble you up all on my own. The best thing for you to do now is to treat yourself to a soothing bath. I'll call the Rialto and cancel the reservation. Then we'll go out and have a wonderful evening together.'

Nicholas stood up.

Patrick began to laugh. 'Poor Ronnie! Oh my dear, what a heavenly situation. Just think how upset he'd be if he ever found out about this. The wicked thing. It would teach him to be kind to my friends.'

'But he'll never find out will he?' said Nicholas anxiously.

'Secrets have a horrid habit of leaking out in London, my dear,' said Patrick.

SIX

MICHAEL sat on a tubular-steel chair in one of the waiting-rooms. There was nothing to read except the morning edition of the *Gladiator* lying on the contemporary table. It hadn't taken him long to glance through it. In the distance he could hear the clatter of typewriters. He grew more and more impatient.

He wondered what Christopher would say when he woke to find himself alone in his pig-sty. It should be just about now that he would be going into the studio to find it deserted. Silly Christopher! The silliest of the whole bunch. Yet quite the most honest, except for Lily.

Lily had proved a bitter disappointment. Such a mouse. It had been like going to bed with a corpse. Every ounce of vitality must have been squeezed out of her long ago by Ronnie. When he had taken her downstairs and put her in a taxi, he had known that there would never be another assignation.

'Will you come with me please, sir.'

Michael followed the messenger along the corridor into an office where he was handed over to a girl wearing glasses.

'Your name, please?' she asked.

'Michael Henry for the seventh time.'

She beckoned him to follow her. They went into the adjoining room where there was a thick carpet on the floor and two secretaries busy at their typewriters. She pressed down the switch on the intercommunication set on the desk and said: 'Mr Henry's here, sir.'

'Send him in,' said Stuart Andrews.

She pointed to the door facing him. He crossed the room and pushed it open. As he closed it behind him he heard her call out: 'You should have knocked first, Mr Henry!'

He found himself in a long room. At the far end he saw Andrews behind a large steel desk.

'I can give you three minutes,' said Andrews. 'You're a friend of Patrick's, I believe.'

'Not exactly a friend.'

'Never mind that. Did you know he asked me to fix you a job?'

'Yes. It was most considerate of him.'

'Don't worry, son. He had his reasons.' He picked up a sheet of paper on which Michael had written his particulars, while he had been waiting. 'Henry, Michael. Born '35 . . . Never mind the school . . . Joined R.A.F. '55 . . . Pilot . . . Grounded for dangerous flying '57. Dangerous flying, eh?'

'I flew under a bridge.'

'Why?'

'I felt like it.'

'So they chucked you out.'

'I've written that down too.'

'I can read, son. As long as you can fly that's all that matters to me. Nothing against high spirits. But don't do it again if you want to stay working for me. Now get down to Blackbushe right away. Report at our office and ask for Fenwick. I've spoken to him on the blower. He doesn't like the sound of you, but he'll take you on if you can fly. He'll try you out today.'

'Fenwick? Isn't he the chap who . . . ?'

'I know, son. Any questions? Right. Away you go.'

Michael said: 'What about the pay?'

'Quite right to mention it. The kind of question I like to hear. Fenwick will give you the dope. If you work you won't go short of money.'

'Thanks very much. I didn't know one could fall into a job as easily as this.'

Andrews smiled for the first time. 'You don't know a thing, son.'

Patrick put down his cup of coffee, stood up and brushed the crumbs off his trousers. 'Have you had enough to eat? Is there anything else you'd like? A delicious peach? A few grapes?'

'No thank you, Patrick,' said Nicholas. 'I couldn't bear to see that waiter again. He embarrasses me.'

'Do you mean Freddie? He's rather sweet.'

'I loathe him.'

'But why? How extraordinary you are. He's such a charming young man. I particularly like the smell of the stuff he puts on his hair.'

'I dread to think what it is.'

'I do believe you're becoming a snob, my dear. You're not just a little bit afraid of the working classes, are you?'

'Of course not.'

'Don't be, my dear. They're such fun. So unrepressed.'

'Talking about work,' said Nicholas. 'You will remember to speak to Ronnie about me, won't you?'

'Of course I will. If he doesn't mend his ways we'll pop you into the editorial chair and have him running round making the tea. I can't imagine what got into him to refuse to see you yesterday.'

'He knew you were away.'

'That's nothing to do with it. He agreed that you should work for *Eleven*. If there's no work, he must make some for you. That was no excuse for such bad manners.'

'You won't say a word to him about Michael, will you?' said Nicholas. 'He would only blame me for letting them come here.'

'Not so much as a whisper, little one. Can I give you a lift anywhere?'

'Which way are you going?'

'I've got to call in at the bank first and see if they'll let me have any money.'

'I'll come with you,' said Nicholas. 'You can drop me off afterwards. There are one or two things that I've got to buy. Shall we meet for lunch?'

'I'm afraid not. Apart from seeing Ronnie I've got one or two other not quite so exciting things to do.'

'Then I shall have to lunch alone,' said Nicholas.

'Ring up your chum Michael. Just think what fun it'll be having lunch with him when he doesn't know that you've told me what a naughty boy he's been. You might even try to frighten him a little.'

'I don't want to.'

'Then you're denying yourself one of the major pleasures of life. There was a philosopher, I can't remember his name, who said that knowledge is power. He was quite right. You ought to try it some time.'

When the car stopped outside the bank, Patrick got out. Nicholas remained seated in the corner.

'Aren't you coming in?' asked Patrick.

'I'll wait here.'

'You'd better come. I might need help. I always feel so frightened in banks.'

As they went inside he took Nicholas's arm, but when they reached the desk Nicholas disengaged himself and wandered away to look at the pictures hanging on the walls. The portly governors of the bank looked at him with serious economic eyes.

Patrick put away his note case and came over to him.

'What's the matter? Don't you like it here?' he asked.

'I was admiring these pillars of society.'

'Aren't they grim? They look so rich. If you don't like them, my dear, I'd better go somewhere else. I'm sure you've got a smart little bank tucked away somewhere which would suit me.'

'I haven't got a bank.'

'How do you live? Or am I being stupid again? We'll put that right for you in no time. Where would you like to open an account? The Bank of England? Coutts? That would be rather smart. Ronnie would be very jealous.'

When they reached the door he stopped and took out his note case. 'Meanwhile you must have something to live on. We can't have you going around like a vagrant. How much would you like?'

'I don't know.'

'How difficult you are. If I don't lend you enough you'll accuse me of being mean.'

Nicholas took him by the arm and hurried him down the steps into the car.

'I wish you wouldn't do that in public,' he said. 'It makes me feel uncomfortable.'

'You are funny. It's much more sensible to borrow money openly. It's only when you're furtive that it's slightly squalid.'

'Could I borrow ten pounds?'

'That won't be nearly enough. I want you to have a good morning and enjoy yourself thoroughly. Go and buy yourself a lovely lot of new clothes. It'll make up for having to lunch all on your own. You must have heaps of parcels to keep you company.'

He handed Nicholas a pile of notes.

'While you're enjoying yourself you might keep your eye out for a suitcase. That travelling kind with hangers fixed inside them are always useful. But I should keep off pigskin. I have a feeling it's slightly vulgar these days.'

'I don't need one.'

'You never know. It's always wise to be prepared to travel. It eliminates those tiresome last-minute rushes.'

Nicholas got out of the car at the corner of Bond Street.

'I'll see you later this afternoon at the flat. Have a good time, Patrick,' he said.

'I'm sure I will, little one.'

*

Patrick watched Nicholas walk away and told the chauffeur to take him to the *Gladiator*.

What a sudden capitulation it had been! In all his vast experience he had never met anyone who had put up such a stubborn defence, only to drop it so suddenly. It was difficult to believe that only yesterday he had gone to Paris quite expecting to find Nicholas flown on his return, or his resistance so impregnable that he would have been forced to abandon an unprofitable siege. For Nicholas had given every indication that he was going to be tiresome and stupid. Perhaps stupid wasn't the right word. On the whole, Nicholas was more intelligent than he had first suspected. He was extremely *naif* like all young men from the provinces. He had a faint touch of idealism about him. It was sad to see it disappear so quickly.

The gods had been on Patrick's side. It had been a magnificent stroke of fortune that it had been raining in Paris the day before. But he had to admit to himself that it wasn't only the weather that had brought him back to England. He hadn't been altogether happy about the prospect of losing Nicholas so quickly. As one grew older one attached more importance to one's successes. It took longer to get over one's failures.

He was going to have no more nonsense from Nicky, who was going to keep him entertained for the next year or eighteen months. Nicholas had a great future in front of him even if he didn't know it. He was going to a very good school. It was fascinating to speculate how he would turn out. Would he be a second Stuart? Would be grow indolent and fat like Ronnie?

It was strange to think that Ronnie had once looked like Nicholas. Young and slim. No. Never slim. There had always been that middle-aged spread lurking in the foreground. What was he now? A chimpanzee. Rather a vicious chimpanzée at times. There had been no occasion for him to insult Nicholas. The trouble was that he was jealous. But he ought to take the trouble to conceal it. His treatment of Nicholas had been positively barbaric.

As the car went down Fleet Street Patrick thought about Stuart. Dear Stuart. He was different. That was on account of his background. Stuart came of peasant stock. Peasants in their stolid way never forgot to be grateful. The contrast between Ronnie and Stuart amused Patrick. The one brilliant, indolent, unhappy and unsuccessful: the other philistine, energetic, happy, ruling from his palace of lies millions of apathetic minds.

Patrick ignored the commissionaire on the door and walked past him into the lift. As it ascended he thought again of Nicholas. He hoped he was buying the right kind of clothes. He really ought to have gone with him. He might turn up in some ghastly off-the-peg bookmaker's pin stripe. It would be so embarrassing to explain to him just why it wouldn't do.

He made his way along the corridor, to the outer office. Without waiting for the secretary to announce him he crossed the room and walked into Stuart's office.

'Good morning, Stuart.'

'Hullo, Alcibiades. Sit down. What can I do for you? I can give you five minutes. Have a cigar.'

'Really, Stuart, I wish you'd collect your wits more quickly and remember who I am. It's so tiresome having to hear the same performance every time I come to the lie factory.'

He sat down in the steel chair and adjusted the creases in his trousers.

'How's the rag prospering?'

Stuart finished lighting his cigar.

'Couldn't be better. Circulation still going up. Here. Take a look at last week's figures.'

'What an appalling reflection on the female intelligence,' said Patrick.

'Every housemaid and whore in the land reads the *Gladiator*,' said Stuart.

'I've got just the man for you, Stuart,' said Patrick. 'Do you remember Ronnie Gras?'

'Gras? One of our fashion designers, isn't he? Bit of a pansy. Friend of all that foreign crowd. Wait a minute. That's right. Offered him a job once. Turned it down. Took him a bloody long time to make up his mind.'

'Do you still want him?'

'What's the idea? I'll buy it.'

'If you want him you can have him. At a price of course. But you'll have to handle him gently.'

'Of course I want him. Designed the Gras look, didn't he? He'd be a hell of a draw on the woman's page. Yes, sir. They'd be mad for him.'

'I suggest you telephone him some time today. But not before midday. Naturally you'll have to make your offer most attractive.'

'What do you get out of this?'

'Nothing, Stuart. But you might remember that if by any chance Nicholas Milestone should come round for that job you so kindly offered him, you're no longer interested. I believe he was meant to be here last Monday. Just tell him he's left it too late.'

'You old sod. You don't want me to bitch up the other kid while you're about it? He's been in this morning. I fixed the job for him.'

'It was kind of you to take the trouble. One should do one's best for these misfits.'

'Stuff it.'

Patrick sighed and stood up. Stuart got up from his desk and conducted him to the door.

'That's much better,' said Patrick. 'I much prefer you when you forget your gladiatorial manners.'

'We understand one another, sweetheart. I never forget my friends.'

'How charming.'

'Care to come down to my new place on the river one week-end? Bring whom you like. Do what you like.'

'I never go near the river,' said Patrick. 'Besides, I don't think I shall be staying in England very much longer.'

It was just as well to have Michael well out of the way, thought Patrick as he came out of the *Gladiator* building. He had a very bad effect on Nicholas besides a nasty habit of looking beyond one's actions and putting his fingers on one's motives. It had been a brilliant idea to tempt him back to his beastly aeroplanes. They should mop up his surplus energy. As long as he stayed with Christopher he was a menace. Christopher with his sentimental stupidity was incapable of realizing how dangerous he could be. Christopher must be made to disgorge him.

While he was being driven to Ronnie's house, he wondered what sort of approach would prove the most amusing. He certainly wasn't going to say to Ronnie outright: 'I'm terribly sorry to have to tell you that Lily's been to bed with Michael.' It would be more subtle than that. He would begin with the smallest prick of the pin. There was no hurry to turn the knife in the wound.

Patrick felt particularly in the mood to torment Ronnie. He was most grateful to Nicholas for handing him such an efficient instrument of torture. On the steps of Ronnie's house he felt dizzy with excitement.

Through the downstairs windows he noticed a bowl of roses standing on a table in the drawing-room. Roses at this time of year! It was monstrous the rate at which Ronnie lived.

He pressed the bell. Lily opened the door.

'Good morning, my dear. Is Ronnie up yet?' asked Patrick.

'Oh no, Patrick. But he's finished breakfast. Would you like to go up?'

Patrick glanced round the hall. It had been altered since his last visit to the house. 'What's happened to our naked friend under the chandelier?' he asked.

'Ronnie had it taken away yesterday. He's found something he likes better,' said Lily. 'I believe it's by Rodin. I expect he'll want to tell you all about it himself.'

A Rodin indeed, thought Patrick as he climbed the stairs. Ronnie's extravagance was becoming maniacal. He couldn't afford to run the house let alone fill it up with expensive chunks of statuary. So that's what had happened to the cheque he had given him for the first number of *Eleven*. He'd be asking for more within a week. *Eleven* looked like being an expensive hobby. He could hear Ronnie say: 'But you see, Patrick, as editor of *Eleven* I've got a position to keep up. You wouldn't want me to live like Christopher, would you?'

Patrick reached the landing, paused and tip-toed along the passage. The door of Ronnie's room was ajar.

Ronnie was lying on his back in the four poster with the eiderdown drawn up under his chin.

Patrick was about to knock on the door, when Ronnie slowly stretched out his hand to the bowl of peaches on the bedside table. Patrick could see his fingers squeezing the fruit to find one that was perfectly ripe. When he had chosen one that met with his approval, he held it in front of his eyes revolving it slowly. He placed it against his nose, sniffed it, and dropped it whole into his mouth. From where he was standing Patrick could see Ronnie's blown-out cheeks.

Ronnie started to masticate slowly. The juice dribbled out of the corners of his mouth. Without moving he blew the stone across the room. It hit the wall and fell to the floor. He closed his eyes and let out a satisfied sigh. His eyes closed. For a moment Patrick thought he was about to fall asleep. But his hand moved out again towards the bowl.

Patrick stood still. Enraptured, he watched the performance being repeated. This time the stone hit one of the posters of the bed and fell on to the eiderdown.

Patrick waited until Ronnie had dropped the third peach into his mouth. Before Ronnie had had time to swallow it, Patrick walked quickly into the room.

'Good morning, my dear. Forgive me for disturbing your beauty sleep,' he said.

Ronnie opened his mouth. Patrick saw the pale pink skin of the peach between his teeth. Ronnie turned away, put his hand over his mouth and spat the peach out under the eiderdown. It rolled along the sheet and fell to the floor.

'You should have eaten it,' said Patrick. 'Now you've wasted it.'

'It doesn't matter,' said Ronnie. He put out his hand to take another one. Remembering that Patrick was watching him, he withdrew it and placed it beneath the bedclothes.

'They're Neapolitan,' he said. 'Too variable to be really good.'

'What a pity!' said Patrick. 'I was sure they were your favourites.'

Ronnie looked at Patrick. 'What are you doing here anyway? I was just about to get up. If you'll wait downstairs I'll join you in about half an hour.'

'I shan't keep you a minute.'

'It's too early to talk,' said Ronnie.

'Not quite twelve. I'm sorry to disturb you so early. I happened to be passing and I suddenly remembered there was something I had to say to you.'

Ronnie felt nervous. He knew that Patrick never paid calls without a purpose. He was looking far too happy. That was a bad sign. As if that wasn't enough he had recognized the ominous mockery in his voice. Patrick was building up for something particularly unpleasant.

Ronnie tried to be charming. He had learnt from experience that flattery sometimes succeeded with Patrick.

'Thank you so much for the flowers you sent yesterday,' he said. 'They are superb. Do have a look at them when you go down and tell me if you approve of Lily's arrangement. You've got such a wonderful knack yourself.'

'Flowers, Ronnie?'

'The roses. I'm afraid I didn't altogether understand the message you sent with them.'

'Nor do I. I certainly never sent you any roses. Are you sure they were for you?'

'Whom else would they be for?'

'They might have been delivered to the wrong house.' He paused. 'They might even have been for Lily.'

'Nonsense,' said Ronnie. He was so surprised by Patrick's suggestion that his hand shot out from under the bedclothes and closed round another peach.

'I'm sure that's the answer,' said Patrick. 'They must have been for Lily.'

'Nonsense,' repeated Ronnie. 'Nobody would send her flowers.'

'You *are* growing old, my dear. Just a weeny bit careless too.'

Ronnie sat up in bed.

'What ludicrous pyjamas!' exclaimed Patrick. 'You look like a wicked old convict.'

'They're Sulka's. . . . Who do you think would send flowers to Lily?'

'How should I know? I don't know who her boy friends are. I merely suggested that they might not have been for you.'

'You *look* as if you know who sent them,' said Ronnie.

Patrick turned and glanced at himself in the mirror. 'I *look* rather well this morning as a matter of fact. Now lie down like a good boy. Have another peach and listen to what I've come to tell you.'

Ronnie lay back in bed.

'I want to talk to you about *Eleven*, my dear,' said Patrick. He paused to savour the gleam of anxiety that sprang into Ronnie's eye. 'I think we're both being rather stupid, my dear. After giving it some thought I've come to the conclusion that I've treated you rather badly.'

Ronnie smiled.

He's like a child, thought Patrick. Scold him and his face puckers up as if he's about to cry; be kind to him and he gurgles with pleasure.

'The trouble is that we've overloaded *Eleven*,' continued Patrick. 'Someone's got to go. The question is who?'

Ronnie kept quiet. Had Patrick called to tell him that Lily couldn't work for *Eleven*?

'No suggestions?' said Patrick. 'I'll have to make them in that case. But if you heard what the younger generation said about you I don't think you'd take so long to make up your mind.'

'What are they saying?'

'I hesitate to repeat it. It makes my ears burn.'

'I don't believe it.'

'That's just another proof that you're growing old, my dear. The younger generation never respects the older. It uses it. Would you call it respectful to refer to you as an old *chimpanzee*?'

'I'm not a chimpanzee. Who calls me a chimpanzee?' said Ronnie.

'You're not to be angry or say anything to him about it. He'd never forgive me,' said Patrick. 'I'm afraid it's Nicholas's invention.'

'It's outrageous. I suppose Michael has a label for me too?'

'They both call you a chimpanzee as far as I know. Michael's done something far worse. I wasn't going to tell you, but I think it would be best if you heard the worst. I'm afraid there's a connection between Michael and the roses.'

'Why should he send me roses?'

'He didn't, my dear. He sent them to Lily.'

'Patrick, you've come here with the deliberate intention of upsetting me,' said Ronnie.

'You've got to listen to me, my dear. It's far better that you should hear these things from an old friend. I'm afraid, Ronnie, I notice a great many things that you miss. At your dinner party it was obvious to me that Michael was paying more attention to Lily than normal manners required. I didn't like the way he was out of the drawing-room for so long.'

'He wasn't accustomed to such rich food. I expect he drank too much. None of them can drink like gentlemen these days.'

'You may be right, my dear. Still, Nicholas tells me that he spent quite a time in the pantry with Lily.'

So many possibilities flooded into Ronnie's mind that he was unable to speak. He blinked, opened his mouth, and waited for Patrick to continue.

'I can see that I've said quite enough already. I thought I ought to warn you. Our generation must stick together. . . . This brings me back to what I was originally going to say to you. I don't think that either Nicholas or Michael are suitable for *Eleven*.'

'Patrick, do you think that young man's trying to cuckold me?' interrupted Ronnie.

'What a charming word! It reminds me of spring. That, my dear, is a question that only Lily can answer. Of course you may decide to say nothing. For your information I happen to know that Michael's got a job today. I don't think we shall be seeing very much of him in the future. . . . Which reminds me. I'm thinking of going away myself for a little while. Nicholas badly needs a holiday.'

'What about *Eleven*?'

'I leave it entirely to you. I think it would be much better that way. I'll stay right in the background as I intended to do originally. It was a mistake to mix business and pleasure.'

'I don't believe you're interested in it any longer.'

'I'm always interested in you, my dear. That's why I've trekked half way across London this morning. I know you'd do the same for me. There's nothing more maddening than to be laughed at by the young. Except, I suppose, to be cuckolded by them.'

He walked towards the door and turned. Ronnie was lost in thought. The loose flesh on his forehead was puckered into ridges. His hand moved towards the bowl of fruit. His fingers closed round the last peach. He dug his nails into it, and with a moan of fury hurled it across the room. It splashed against the window.

'Lily! Lily!' he shouted.

Patrick slipped quietly out of the room. He passed Lily running up the stairs. How right he had been not to tell Ronnie everything. Lily would deny it. It would take Ronnie a long time to get over his doubts.

It had been a brilliant piece of improvisation to make use of the roses. It had fitted in perfectly after the remark about the chimpanzee. That had been an insult to his vanity which would hurt him far more than the discovery of Lily's lapse. Everything was working out precisely as he had planned. Ronnie had been put in his place for insulting Nicholas; Michael was out of the way in case he should influence Nicholas. Nicholas should now prove manageable. He was isolated. He couldn't escape to the *Gladiator*. There was no job for him on *Eleven*. He might go back to Rochester. That was extremely unlikely. He had tasted a new life. He seemed to like it.

Patrick told the chauffeur to take him to the Fulham Road. As he started to climb the steps of Christopher's house, the front door opened.

'Hullo, Patrick,' said Christopher. 'I was looking out of the window and saw your monstrous car coming down the street. I came down to let you in so all my neighbours will know what rich friends I've got. You haven't got Michael hidden in the back somewhere, have you?'

'I'm afraid not.'

'Oh dear. I wonder where he can be. I haven't seen him all morning. There was just a chance that he might be with you.'

They were still standing in the doorway. Christopher peered anxiously down the street.

'May I come up?' asked Patrick.

'My manners always disappear when I'm unhappy,' said Christopher. 'It's terribly untidy upstairs although I know you don't mind the way I live even though you live so differently yourself. You're not like Ronnie. He thinks that artists should live in palaces and be pensioned off by the state at ten thousand a year.'

As they went upstairs Patrick said: 'How's the portrait progressing?'

'We've completed the sittings. But I don't want you to see it until it's finished. You're so critical. If you were unkind about it now, I might abandon it for ever.'

'How sensitive you are, Christopher!'

They went into the studio. Patrick noticed that the canvas had been taken off the easel and placed facing the wall.

'Shall I make you some tea? Or would you like some lemonade?' said Christopher.

Patrick shook his head.

Christopher moistened his fingers in his mouth, dipped them into a tin of lemonade powder perched on the arm of the chair, and started to lick them.

'Sure you won't change your mind? It's terribly good,' he said.

'Quite certain. May I sit down?'

Christopher spread a newspaper over the dilapidated armchair. 'There. I don't think your suit will get dirty now. Michael's always complaining about the dirt. Oh dear, I wish you'd brought me news of him.'

'Didn't he say where he was going?'

'I haven't seen him since late last night,' said Christopher. 'He comes and goes at all kinds of odd hours. But it was strange for him to get up and disappear so early this morning without saying anything.'

'You've been very kind to him,' said Patrick.

'I've done what I could,' said Christopher. 'He's so terribly neurotic although he doesn't know it himself. I don't know whether I ought to tell you, Patrick, but I think he's slightly mad.'

'I know.'

'You didn't know,' said Christopher. 'Nobody knew except me.'

'My dear Christopher, don't upset yourself. It was obvious to anyone the first time they met Michael that he was *odd* to say the least of it.'

'I'll tell you something you don't know,' said Christopher. 'He carries a gun about with him the whole time. A real one. He's got bullets for it too.'

'I'm not surprised. He's utterly psychopathic. I can't see what you hope to do about it.'

'I don't know. I thought just being near him and trying to help him might be of some use to him.'

Patrick looked at Christopher and smiled: 'All I can say, my dear, is you've failed lamentably. I can't help agreeing with Ronnie at times. You should be forcefully prevented from good works.'

'Oh dear. What have I done now? I know. I can feel it. You've come here to torment me.'

'Do sit down. You look like something in the zoo pacing up and down.'

Christopher collapsed on the divan and sat rubbing his large hands together. Patrick looked at him with disgust. Did Christopher ever grasp what went on round him? Did he ever know what he was doing? He was sitting like a naughty boy waiting to be punished. He looked as if he were longing to be hurt. It was nauseating the way he allowed himself to be mocked and bullied. Why did he never try to protect himself? It was irritating enough to have to admit that he had an enormous talent. But that it should reside in someone so weak-willed and intellectually stupid was too much to bear.

Christopher was unable to sit still. He crossed and uncrossed his long legs. His foot caught against a cup lying on the floor. It was already cracked and fell to pieces. He knelt down and started to collect the fragments in his paint-stained hands. He looked at Patrick with the melancholy eyes of a dog.

'I'm ever so sorry. How careless of me,' he said. 'You've made me terribly nervous. There's something forbidding about you this morning. It's almost as if you have the evil eye.'

He got up off his knees, looking round for somewhere to put the broken pieces. The waste paper basket was filled already and overflowing. He dropped them in the grate.

'I'm afraid it's terribly dirty in here,' he said.

'For goodness' sake stop being afraid for one minute,' said Patrick.

He looked round the studio with visible distaste at the debris in the grate, the pieces of china, the torn-up letters which had blown on to the edge of the mat, and two crushed roses lying behind the fire bars. Roses. The same coloured roses as he'd seen at Ronnie's house. His shot in the dark had been absolutely right. They had come from Michael.

'I see you've been cultivating roses,' he said.

Christopher smiled weakly. 'So Nicholas told you, did he? I can't help it even if you do think it was a terrible waste of money on my part. I couldn't stop myself.'

'Of course you couldn't. You always do things without thinking, my dear.'

'It wasn't so wrong as you may think. To begin with the woman I bought them from was terribly pleased. She needed the money more than I did. When Mikey suggested taking them to the hospital I knew it had all been pre-ordained. It was a wonderful idea. It's awful to think that there are children who have never seen a rose.'

With difficulty Patrick prevented himself from laughing. 'I forgot you were so fond of children, my dear,' he said.

'You knew how much I always wanted to have children, Patrick. That's one of the reasons I got married, even though I knew at the time I'd be a very bad father. I was frightened of failing as an artist and I thought there'd be sufficient compensation in becoming a father.'

'You failed in that. But you succeeded as an artist.'

'That's why I shall never marry again. There's no need. It isn't vital any longer to have children. I've grown far too selfish.'

'I'm sure you haven't. Not everybody would have bought roses like that. *Au fond* you're generous. That's why anybody can make a fool of you.'

He looked down at the dust which had settled on his shoes during the few minutes he had been in the studio.

'I'm afraid people do make a fool of me,' said Christopher. 'I don't mind. If it gives them pleasure I'm pleased to be of use to them.'

'Presumably you'll be delighted to hear that Michael gave your roses to Lily. He never went near a hospital,' said Patrick.

The effect of his words was fascinating. Christopher's expression took a few seconds to alter. He had been grinning in his imbecile way, displaying his discoloured teeth, as Patrick had begun to speak. When he had finished he was still smiling. Then slowly the colour began to go out of his cheeks. His mouth stayed open. It started to open and close like the gills of a fish out of water.

Patrick looked at his eyes. They had begun to moisten in the corners.

'Oh! That was very wicked of him,' Christopher said very quietly. He looked sadly at Patrick. 'Why did he tell you? If one's done something wrong it's better to keep it to oneself and let one's own conscience punish one.'

'I happened to find out by chance,' said Patrick.

'I wish you'd never told me. Now I shall never be able to talk to him without feeling embarrassed. I could never bring myself to reproach him. It would only make him even more bitter. He'd accuse me of spying on him and trying to organize his life.'

'I shouldn't worry, my dear. I have a feeling that he won't be coming back.'

Christopher, who had got up from the divan, sat down again quickly.

'He's gone back to his aeroplanes,' said Patrick. 'Nicholas told me he's got himself a job with a private airline.'

'He never said a word to me about it,' said Christopher. 'That was most unkind of him. Most unkind. The idea is absolute madness.'

'You said yourself he's mad.'

'That's why he should have told me. I'd have done everything to dissuade him. His future doesn't lie in the past. His future is the future.'

'How madly acute!'

'It's all very well for you to laugh. You never look beyond people. You're not interested in discovering what motivates them.'

'You're so wrong. Though I must say that what one finds is usually too depressing for words.'

'I suppose you know what's made Michael do this?'

'Of course. First of all he doesn't like charity. He wants to stand on his own. The poor boy hasn't the faintest idea of how to set about it. He resents the fact that we're established in our various ways. So he hates us. It's a kind of jealousy. I'm afraid he hates you too, my dear.'

'Why didn't he tell me so?' said Christopher.

'He did. I don't see how he could have said more plainly what he thought of us all. He singled Ronnie out in particular. He more or less defecated on his doorstep. It's placed us all in a very tricky position. Ronnie's not going to like you at all for harbouring such a viper and failing to keep it under proper control.'

'What did he do?' asked Christopher.

'He popped Lily into bed. I can't say how much your roses contributed to his success.'

Christopher did not reply. He walked to the window and looked down into the street.

'I'm afraid he's had a good laugh at our expense,' said Patrick. 'In many ways he wasn't quite such a fool as you seem to think,

Christopher. He's succeeded in leaving quite a mess behind. Ronnie's very cross with you. He's going to be just as angry with me when he discovers exactly what happened. Which means he's not going to hear of Nicholas working for *Eleven*. I'm beginning to wonder what's going to happen to that little venture.'

Without turning round Christopher said: 'Please go away, Patrick.'

'Of course. I'm sorry to have brought you such depressing news, my dear.' He paused, hoping that Christopher would turn and face him. Christopher did not move. 'I can't tell you how sorry I am about it all,' he went on. 'But it's always best to face the truth. I know how much you value truth, my dear. Are you going to let me out?'

Christopher shook his head. He kept his face close to the window, determined that Patrick should not see the tears in his eyes.

Ronnie closed his eyes and leant back against the pillows exhausted. What he had always dreaded had finally occurred. The only consolation was that no greater calamity could now befall him. He felt rather hungry.

He could hear Lily crying. He opened his eyes and said: 'Why did you have to deceive me? You know you're free to come and go as you please.'

Lily wiped her eyes. 'I know. I thought you'd be miserable if I'd told you.'

'Are you in love with the boy?'

'Oh no, Ronnie. I've told you what happened. He just made me feel young.'

'The inference is plain. I don't,' said Ronnie bitterly.

'Please don't say that. It isn't of any importance to me any longer. I only wanted to prove something to myself. I shall never see him again.'

'You don't want to leave me?'

'Oh, no, Ronnie.'

'Then you'd better go down and see about lunch. I don't know whether I shall be able to eat much. You've probably ruined my digestion. You'd better concoct some particularly light and appetizing dishes.'

Alone in the bedroom Ronnie's anger faded. It was only when one was suspicious that one could feel angry. Lily had made no attempt to lie to him. He was civilized and no civilized man tormented himself over the inexplicable psychology of women. What really mattered was that Lily still loved him. He had to admit that it was true that he had paid insufficient attention to her. He had begun to take her for granted. He had grown careless in his middle age. Along had come this insolent young man and thrown himself at her. She hadn't stood a chance.

He put on his dressing gown and went into the bathroom.

After all, he told himself, as he lay in the hot bath, we attach a ridiculous importance to infidelity. It wasn't the act of infidelity that made a man miserable when his wife or mistress was unfaithful to him. It was the fear of being deserted. Of being left alone. Lily had no wish to leave him. He hadn't got to face the appalling prospect of being left alone.

As he made his way down the stairs to lunch, he had made up his mind to forget the incident as quickly as possible. He went into the morning room where Lily was waiting for him. He put his arms round her and kissed her gently on the forehead. 'You're looking very beautiful this morning, my dear,' he said.

He picked up the papers, and settled himself on the sofa in front of the blazing log fire.

He had just finished reading *The Times*' fourth leader when the telephone started to ring.

Lily picked up the receiver.

'Mr Andrews of the *Gladiator* wants to talk to you, Ronnie,' she said.

She brought the telephone across the room, and put it on the arm of the sofa.

'Mr Gras? Andrews here. *Gladiator*. I'll come straight to the point. If you're not engaged at the moment, I can use you.'

'*Use* me?'

'I won't waste time over the details now. I want you to change your mind and take over our woman's page. We'll pay you well. Ten thousand a year and expenses. I'll have a contract sent round to you. Look it over right away, and let me have your comments if any.'

'I'll have to think it over.'

'Sure, sure. Sleep on it for twenty-four hours. I'll ring you tomorrow morning.'

Ronnie replaced the receiver.

'A glass of sherry, dear,' he called.

When Lily had placed the glass in his hand, he noticed that it was shaking.

Ten thousand a year and expenses. Patrick would have to start looking for someone else to edit *Eleven*.

Patrick was exhausted when he arrived at his flat. But it was a pleasant kind of exhaustion.

He had experienced such an enjoyable morning that he decided to break his rule of no spirits before the evening. He mixed himself a martini, and lay down on the sofa under the window.

There was no longer any point in staying in England. *Eleven* would never materialize now. The most sensible thing to do was to go away as soon as possible. Nicholas certainly deserved a holiday. Where could they go? North Africa? No. Rather too dangerous. In spite of all the money they were spending on pacifying the place, the French seemed to be having no success at all. There was a new hotel in Bermuda that people were talking about. One was likely to meet too many of one's old friends there. It would be just as well to keep Nicholas away from them. Was a gentle cruise the answer? That meant meeting the most dreadful people. Cruises were no longer possible. They'd been taken up by business men from the Midlands with their wives. What was the name of his friend who had an island in the Aegean? That was no good. The Greeks didn't love the English at the moment. Why couldn't people stop bickering and live in peace?

Patrick decided to leave the problem of where to go to Nicholas. He might have a brilliant idea. Young men usually had some place in their dreams where they longed to go. If Nicholas proved unoriginal they could always go to Paris first, and decide there where to go.

He finished his drink, put his feet up on the sofa, lay back and closed his eyes.

He was asleep when Nicholas came into the flat. He awoke to hear him moving about in the hall before coming into the sitting-room.

'Hullo, my dear. Did you have a lovely time shopping?'

'Yes. How did you get on?'

'Splendidly. But you must tell me first exactly what you've been doing. Did you buy everything you wanted?'

'I seem to have spent an awful lot of money.'

'Quite right. It's such fun, isn't it? Did you have a delicious lunch?'

'I tried the Ritz.'

'Oysters and champagne?'

'How did you guess?'

'Intuition.'

'Did you talk to Ronnie?'

'For a few minutes. I spent most of the morning with Christopher. You know how long it takes to get away from him.'

'Is it all right about *Eleven*? I mean, you've fixed it all up with Ronnie.'

'Everything's been decided, my dear. . . . What have you done with all those exciting parcels?'

'I've left them in the hall.'

'Did you find a suitcase?'

'I'm afraid not. All *the possible* ones turned out to be pigskin. . . . Tell me more about Ronnie. What did he decide I could do?'

Patrick patted the sofa. 'Come and sit by me. I'm afraid you're not going to like me very much. You mustn't blame me. I did everything I could for you, but Ronnie refused to listen to me. I'm afraid he's terribly conservative. The fact is, my dear, he was most uncomplimentary about you; almost rude when I mentioned your name.'

'You told him about Michael and Lily!' exclaimed Nicholas. 'You promised you'd never say a word.'

'I swear I didn't. He found out for himself. I'm afraid that naughty girl was smitten with remorse and told him everything.'

'What am I going to do?' said Nicholas.

'*Do*? I don't see why you have to *do* anything except look delicious. That doesn't require very much effort, does it?'

'This is terrible. I can't spend all my time doing nothing,' said Nicholas.

'Let's forget about it for the moment, my dear. I'm sure something will turn up. Besides, I've a nasty feeling that we've been through all this before. Worrying ages you, my dear. You mustn't forget that. You almost talk as if it's my fault that Ronnie doesn't like you. I think his behaviour's childish in the extreme, but there it is. I'm afraid you must blame your friend Michael if Ronnie isn't exactly anxious to have you on *Eleven*. Not that I think it matters nearly as much as you seem to think. It's not as if you've been wasting your time since you came to London. I mean, you're much more of a man of the world now than you were a week ago. You have enjoyed the last few days, haven't you? You haven't been bored, and that's what really matters.'

'I've had a marvellous time,' said Nicholas. 'The only thing that worries me is that I seem to have lost control of myself. Please don't think I'm blaming you, Patrick. You've been so kind to me.'

'I'm glad about that. It was rather naughty of me to throw you at my friends so quickly. I can see now it must have been a ghastly ordeal. Let's forget all about it and pretend you've just arrived at the station looking anxious and rather lost.'

'I don't want to put the clock back,' said Nicholas, 'although the last week has been the most exciting in my life.'

He was speaking the truth. The last week had made his former life seem dull and dreary. He was appalled by the poverty of his existence in Rochester. Now he could buy what he liked; eat where he chose. He wondered how he had been able to tolerate provincial life for so long.

Patrick said: 'We must have lots more fun together. What do you think we should do now? Where would you like to go?'

'Couldn't we stay here for a little while. I'm rather tired.'

'I meant where would you like to go for a holiday, my dear,' said Patrick. 'If you're tired it's high time you left this boring little island.'

Nicholas knew that he must do what Patrick wanted. On no account must he resist. He remembered what had happened when he had refused to go with him to Paris.

'I'd like to go wherever you want to go,' he said.

'Rather unoriginal, my dear. Never mind. In that case I suggest we go to Paris for a few days. Meanwhile, if you think of some charming corner of the world which I've never seen, perhaps you'll let me know. You ought to have a really long holiday. Would you like to go to the South Seas?'

Nicholas stared at the floor, looked up at Patrick and said: 'It's funny to think within the last two weeks I've lost two jobs I never started. First of all the *Gladiator* and then *Eleven*. Now I'm not going to work at all. I'm going to France on a holiday with you. Usually one doesn't have a holiday until one's done some work.'

'Life so often turns out the opposite to what we expect, my dear. I think it makes it rather intriguing.'

Nicholas said: 'Did you see Michael today?'

'I don't see the connection. What an odd way your mind runs! As a matter of fact I didn't. Christopher hadn't seen him either. He seems to have disappeared.'

'I must see Michael,' said Nicholas.

'You'd better telephone him.'

'I'll wait until tomorrow.'

'You won't have time to go chasing after him tomorrow. I feel we're going to have rather a busy day packing, buying tickets, and finding you a smart new case.'

Nicholas had to see Michael. He had accepted Patrick's terms. He had made a decision and sold himself. Now that he had taken the step, he wanted someone to tell him that he had done the right thing.

'If I won't have time tomorrow I must find him tonight,' he said.

'I don't see why it matters all that much, my dear.'

'I want to say goodbye to him, Patrick. He's my oldest friend. I simply must see him.'

'Must? I've a feeling it's going to be rather difficult,' said Patrick. He stretched out his arms and yawned. 'Do you know, my dear, I'm far more exhausted than I'd imagined. What I need is a hot bath. When I've filled the bath with foam, come and talk to me. I feel like a dryad when it's up to my ears.'

When Patrick came out of the bathroom feeling relaxed and refreshed, Nicholas was no longer in the flat.

Patrick walked into the hall. The parcels lay still unopened on the floor. Nicholas's coat was not hanging among the other coats. Could he have slipped out to buy an evening paper or some cigarettes? It would have been much simpler to order them by telephone. It was the kind of funny thing Nicholas might do. He had not yet learnt the way to live, although he was coming along fast.

Patrick dressed slowly, paying particular attention to his appearance. He returned to the sitting-room and poured himself a drink. He looked at his watch and frowned. Surely it didn't take Nicholas an hour to do whatever he was doing? It was most careless of him not to have left a message where he was going. It was slightly irritating too the way he had declined his invitation to come and talk to him in the bath.

As the minutes passed, Patrick's impatience changed to anger. It was outrageous behaviour. Certainly not a very happy start to a holiday. Nicholas had seemed keen enough about that. What on earth could have possessed him? Michael. That was the answer. Nicholas had rushed off to find Michael. He had even used the word *must*.

Patrick knew that he should have put an end to that nonsense for good. He had been right in supposing that Michael had a most unhealthy influence over Nicholas. Michael was too cynical, too rude. He made no effort to conceal his feelings. It wouldn't surprise him in the least if Michael had already told Nicholas what a dangerous position he was in.

It was now six o'clock. Did Nicholas expect him to wait for him indefinitely?

With an exclamation of anger Patrick went into the bedroom and put on his coat.

When he came out of the lift, he crossed the foyer to the hall porter's desk. 'If anyone calls for me while I'm out, you're to ask them to wait down here,' he said. 'You're to allow no one to go up to my flat. Absolutely no one. Do you understand?'

'Perfectly, sir.'

As Patrick was being driven to the Rialto he grew more and more angry with Nicholas. It was surprising Nicholas hadn't borrowed the car while he was about it. Whatever he was doing, it was extremely ill-mannered to leave one alone so suddenly. Did he really imagine that one could telephone one's friends and say that one had been deserted and couldn't bear to be left alone? Nicholas was taking far too much for granted.

Nicholas searched desperately for a taxi. It seemed to him essential that he should find Michael as quickly as possible. Only a few minutes ago he had been willing to do whatever Patrick wanted. If Patrick had said they were leaving for Timbuktu he would have gone with him without protest. Suddenly the situation had changed. Before he knew what he was doing, he had run out of the flat. Had he resented the casual way in which Patrick had accepted his submission?

Patrick had fanned the dying embers of Nicholas's independence into a final splutter of flames. Instinctive fear had sent him flying out into the street, while the last chance of escape remained.

When he reached Christopher's studio he saw that there was no light shining in the upstairs room. He asked the driver to wait, walked slowly up the steps, and pressed the bell. He heard it ring inside the house. But there was no sound of footsteps descending the stairs. The studio was deserted.

Nicholas's mood began to change. Both Christopher and Michael were out. They might not come back for several hours. He would accomplish nothing sitting on the doorstep waiting for them to return. He had already been away from Patrick far too long. He must think about getting back to him as quickly as possible. He would have to think of a good excuse to explain his sudden disappearance. He could say that he had gone out to buy a paper or some cigarettes. Once again he had acted without thinking. The consequences as usual would be unpleasant.

As he drove back in the taxi, he knew that his excuse was too weak to use. He had been away too long. It might be wiser to try to explain the truth.

He paid off the taxi and ran into the foyer.

'Whom do you want?' called the porter.

'I'm just going up.'

'So I see. Whom do you want?'

'I'm staying here.'

'I don't know anything about that. The gentleman left instructions that if anyone called they were to wait for him down here.'

'How long will he be?'

'How should I know?' said the porter.

Nicholas sat down on a chair and waited. Occasionally the porter sauntered past him to the door, inspected the night, threw a glance in his direction, and returned whistling to his desk to study the next day's racing.

Nicholas waited for two hours. It was finally the look of unconcealed contempt on the porter's face that drove him out. In any case Patrick might not return until the early hours of the morning. There was nothing for Nicholas to do except see about finding himself an hotel for the night. It would be wiser to be out of the way when Patrick returned. He would probably be tired and that would be the worst time to attempt an explanation.

As Nicholas walked out into the street he cursed himself for having behaved so idiotically. He should have thought about the consequences of running out on Patrick without so much as a word of explanation.

The running away had been easy. Getting himself back again might prove difficult.

SEVEN

NICHOLAS woke as soon as it began to grow light. It was too early to get up so he lay in bed watching the sky brighten through the window of the drab hotel bedroom. He wondered whether he should leave the hotel at once and hurry back to Patrick. But so far everything he had done on the spur of the moment had turned out disastrously.

The previous evening it had seemed stupid to wait up all night for Patrick. Now in the growing light of a new day he realized it was exactly what he should have done. It was what Patrick meant him to do. Now it was going to be doubly difficult to explain not only why he had rushed out of the flat, but why he had spent the night at an hotel near Victoria Station.

Perhaps Patrick would refuse to see him. Perhaps he had instructed the porter that he was never to be allowed up. This time he might have to wait about for hours until Patrick happened to come downstairs. What would he do if Patrick refused ever to see him again? He couldn't blame Patrick. His behaviour had been so stupid. Why hadn't he thought of telephoning him the moment he had reached Christopher's studio and found it deserted? Then at least Patrick wouldn't have gone out without leaving a message. Why hadn't he left a note with the porter when he had decided to spend the night at an hotel? When Patrick returned the hall porter would have told him that he had waited in the foyer for two hours. Patrick would have assumed that he couldn't be bothered to wait longer, or that he was trying to show that he didn't care. But he cared desperately.

Nicholas looked round the squalid hotel bedroom and shuddered. This was what he would have to return to. In a moment of thoughtless stupidity he had thrown everything away. The easy life, security and the holiday.

Nicholas was so horrified at the prospect that he got out of bed, dressed hurriedly, and left the hotel. He had to get back to Patrick without further delay. Each minute his position became more precarious; each minute took Patrick farther away from him.

There were no taxis in the street. He was on the point of getting on to a bus, when he changed his mind. Perhaps it would be wiser to telephone Patrick first. He had a vision of being humiliated by the hall porter. He went into a telephone kiosk, dialled the number, and asked to be put through to Patrick.

'I'm sorry,' said the girl on the switchboard. 'He left instructions that no calls were to be put through before eleven.'

'Would you tell him Mr Milestone called, please?'

He came out of the kiosk feeling even more dejected. The only consolation was that by telephoning he had avoided being insulted by the porter. It was eight o'clock. There was nothing he could do for three hours. He prayed that Patrick would sleep until eleven. If he could arrive at the moment Patrick woke and before he had had time to recollect the previous evening, there was still a chance he was not completely lost.

As Nicholas wandered along the street he grew calmer. Perhaps Patrick was as worried as he was. Patrick might be out of his mind with anxiety, imagining him under a bus or lying badly injured in hospital. The more he thought about it, the more likely it seemed.

He was wondering how he could pass the next three hours when he remembered that he had originally set out to see Michael. It was Michael who had caused him to make such a fool of himself.

As he made his way in the direction of Christopher's studio, he began to think the situation absurd. He had been worrying himself unnecessarily. When he reached the studio, he noticed that the curtains were drawn. He ran up the steps and pressed the bell.

The window above his head was opened. Christopher looked out. 'Oh. It's you Nicky,' he called. 'I'll be down in a second.'

When Christopher opened the door, Nicholas was surprised to see that he was already dressed. His hair was unbrushed and he was unshaven. His suit was so crumpled that he looked as if he had slept in it.

'I'm terribly sorry to disturb you at this unearthly hour of the morning,' said Nicholas.

'I'm terribly glad you've come.'

They climbed the stairs to the studio. Christopher went to the window and pulled back the curtain.

'I really came to see Michael,' said Nicholas.

Christopher who was looking up at the sky, turned round and said: 'Haven't you heard?'

'Heard?'

'I'm afraid you can't see Michael, Nicky. You see, he's dead.'

'But I've come to see him,' said Nicholas. He sat down on the chair and stared at Christopher.

'Didn't you see the evening paper yesterday?' said Christopher. 'He was killed in a flying accident. At about three o'clock yesterday afternoon.'

'It wasn't much use my coming here to see him, was it?' said Nicholas.

'When people die it takes a long time to grow accustomed to their absence,' said Christopher.

Nicholas said: 'What happened?'

'You'd better read it yourself,' said Christopher. He knelt down, picked the paper off the floor, and handed it to Nicholas.

'Read it to me,' said Nicholas.

'It's only a small paragraph. It says that Michael Herbert Henry, an ex-R.A.F. pilot, was killed when the plane he was flying crashed into a wood at Blackbushe this afternoon.'

'It doesn't tell us very much, does it?' said Nicholas.

'I went down there straight away. I got there about six o'clock,' said Christopher.

'That's about when I came here,' said Nicholas.

'I saw a man called Fenwick,' continued Christopher. He paused. 'I don't know how to go on.' He felt in his pocket for his handkerchief.

'Have mine,' said Nicholas.

'I'm sorry about this,' said Christopher. He took the handkerchief and dabbed his eyes.

'What did he have to say?'

'He was awfully nice. He's chief pilot to the airline. I can't even remember its name, but it doesn't matter. Apparently Mikey went down yesterday morning to fill a vacancy. Naturally they had to test him to see whether he could still fly all right. First of all he went up with someone else. They flew around for some time, and landed safely. Then Fenwick told Mikey to take off and fly round on his own. Mikey had been flying solo for a quarter of an hour, when Fenwick told him over the radio to come and land. Mikey took no notice of him, but climbed higher and higher. He wouldn't answer the radio. The next thing that Fenwick saw was Mikey's plane diving for the ground.'

'My God!'

'That's about all,' said Christopher. 'Fenwick said it could have been an accident.' He started to cry. He made no effort to wipe away the tears which poured down his cheeks.

Nicholas, who had been staring at the floor, looked for the first time at the easel standing in the centre of the studio.

'I finished it last night when I got back,' said Christopher. 'It's a different picture now. But it's true. Not many people are going to like it.'

'It's wonderful. Just what I thought of him,' said Nicholas.

'He was a nihilist,' said Christopher. 'Last night I painted what I knew in the first place. But I never dared to do it before. Last night there was nothing to stop me. I'd like you to have it, Nicholas. Michael was never a friend of mine. If he cared for anyone except himself it was you. I wasn't any help to him. The night before he went away he said: "I wish to God you'd stop trying to father me. People shouldn't have fathers. Fathers who try to help their sons only succeed in irritating them." I don't believe I can help people, Nicky. I tried with Michael, but only succeeded in making him hate me.'

'He despised everyone,' said Nicholas.

There was silence in the studio. Christopher gave Nicholas back his handkerchief. 'I hope you'll stay for a little while,' he said. 'I should be terribly grateful.'

'As long as you like.'

'That's awfully kind of you. I'm sure we'll be able to help one another. The best thing we can do now is to go and find some breakfast. When one's miserable it's best to eat. If one doesn't, one's physical resistance is lowered.'

As they went down the stairs Nicholas wondered whether he should telephone Patrick.

He decided to wait. Compared with Michael, Patrick seemed unimportant for the moment.

Ronnie Gras woke after a restless night. He had gone early to bed in the hope that a night's rest would help him to make up his mind. He was still angry with himself for having been such a fool as to imagine that Patrick could ever change; that he could do anything without a hidden motive. He had forgotten that Patrick would never have consented to finance *Eleven* unless it was sure to add to his own amusement. Ronnie had been carried away by the idea of *Eleven*. It had seemed the great opportunity. He would prove with *Eleven* that he was not a second-rate failure.

He had dreamt all night about money. As he lay beneath the bedclothes trying to count the shafts of light that were piercing the gaps in the curtains, he was still thinking about money. It was money that had gradually destroyed his integrity. He should never have been a fashion designer. He had given up painting for a quick return. Yet he had never made enough money, probably because he was only capable of spending it. He would have been far happier as a painter. Christopher, in spite of the incredible squalor in which he lived, would ultimately command greater respect. It was a galling thought.

The telephone beside the bed began to ring.

To begin with Ronnie was infuriated, then amazed that anyone should dare to telephone him so early in the morning. He watched Lily sit up in bed, stretch out her hand, and lift the receiver.

'It's Mr Andrews, dear. He wants to speak to you.'

'Tell him I never talk on the telephone before ten.'

'Yes, dear.'

Lily repeated his message. He heard Andrews's voice and a click as he hung up.

Ronnie closed his eyes and sighed. This was just another example of the world's callousness. As if he wasn't already sufficiently tormented on the rack without being pursued into the privacy of his bed. He would like to have told Andrews that he never wanted to hear from him again; that he was wasting his time telephoning. For a moment he thought of asking Lily to call Andrews back and tell him to go to hell. One should use strong language with an iconoclast. The idea gave him immense satisfaction.

'He sounded very angry, dear,' said Lily. 'He couldn't understand why Patrick told him to ring you if you didn't want the job.'

Ronnie sat up in bed.

'Lily,' he said. 'I'll never speak to Patrick again. He's never to come here again. I will not be *sold* by him. He's forbidden my house, do you understand?'

'Whatever you say, dear. What shall I do when Andrews rings up again?'

'Anything you like. Say I've gone to Tibet. No. Tell him to go to hell.'

He collapsed against his pillows delighted with himself. He had defeated Patrick for the first time for years. What was more, quite suddenly he had succeeded in doing something he had failed to do for forty years. He had actually been able to refuse money. It was encouraging to know that there was a level below which he would not sink.

He smiled at Lily. She was looking particularly young and pretty.

Lily put out her hand and stroked the side of his face.

'I'm so glad you refused the *Gladiator*,' she said.

'Why?'

'Because you'll be much happier making a great success of *Eleven*.'

'Please, Lily, don't torment me. I've just said I'll never speak to Patrick again.' He rolled over on to his side away from her.

'Listen, my dear,' said Lily. 'Don't you see that's exactly how Patrick expects you to react. He wants you to abandon *Eleven*. But you mustn't. You're so much cleverer than he is. You mustn't let him win so easily.' Ronnie, who had never heard Lily say so much before, rolled back and stared at her in amazement.

'Say that again,' he said.

'Can't you see, Ronnie? You've got the better of Patrick for the first time in your life by refusing Andrews. Patrick was sure you wouldn't be able to. Now you must go ahead with *Eleven*. With or without Patrick.'

'Do you think I could do it?'

'You're the only person who can.'

'But the money?'

'Ronnie, you are so stupid. Don't you realize that the moment you tell Patrick you don't want his money, he'll be furious. He'll go to any lengths to make you take it.'

Ronnie began to tremble with excitement.

'Lily, you're a genius,' he cried. He sat up in bed. 'Pull the curtains back and let's see what sort of day it is. . . . You've made me feel rather hungry.'

'I'll bring you breakfast,' she said. 'Sussex eggs cooked in Devonshire butter.'

'You're wonderful, Lily,' said Ronnie. 'You shall have your portrait on the cover of the first number of *Eleven*. I'll commission Christopher. I'm going to enjoy my breakfast.'

When Lily reached the door he called out: 'Haven't you got any lamb's kidneys? Just two or three?'

*

As the morning dragged slowly by, Christopher became more and more convinced that he alone had been responsible for Michael's death. At midday he was calling himself a guilty accomplice; at one o'clock a murderer.

'But Christopher, there was nothing more you could have done,' said Nicholas. 'Michael told me himself that he was longing to get away from us all.'

'I knew that too. I was certain he would commit suicide. I should never have left him on his own for a second.'

'If it was suicide, you're not a murderer,' said Nicholas. 'Patrick is if anybody. Even if he acted with the best intentions, fixing Michael up with the job, he'd still be more guilty than you.'

'In that case I should never have allowed him to go near Patrick,' said Christopher. 'He's much too dangerous. A mother who forgets to put up the guard so that her child falls into the flames and is burnt to death, is guilty, isn't she?'

'I suppose so,' said Nicholas. He was beginning to grow tired. He had got up early. He had been listening to Christopher repeating himself for hours. What was the good of arguing with him when all he wanted to be told was that he was guilty of murder?

'There you are,' said Christopher. 'I knew you thought so the whole time. You're trying to be kind to me. I don't want kindness. I want you to speak the truth.'

Nicholas began to feel slightly exasperated. Christopher was making more fuss about Michael than he was himself. Christopher wanted to be in at the death; he wanted to be sure that the whole world would see the blood on his hands. If they didn't see it, they would have to be told about it.

If anyone should be miserable on account of Michael's death, it was himself. But he had reacted quietly. Death was a fact. Weeping for Michael would not bring him back to life, assuming that he wanted to return. Christopher had no right to take upon himself the role of chief mourner. He had hardly known Michael, who had only stayed with him to save himself the expense of an hotel.

Christopher continued to talk, striding up and down the studio. Nicholas paid less and less attention to the stream of self-deprecation. While Christopher rambled on he began to think about his own predicament. Every minute that passed made his future more precarious. He had come to the studio originally to see Michael. If Michael had been there he would have told him not to be such a bloody fool but to get back to Patrick as quickly as possible and get to work with his extractor.

During the last few hours Nicholas had paid little attention to his surroundings. Now the squalor of the studio took on a new significance. He looked at the broken divan, the rubbish piled in the grate, and Christopher in his creased suit and filthy shirt. This was what he feared. Poverty and squalor. In contrast he saw the suite at the Rialto, and Patrick's flat filled with beautiful objects. Every moment that he hesitated the latter was slipping through his fingers.

'Christopher, if you don't mind I must go now,' he said.

Christopher looked at him in surprise. 'Go? Where?'

'Patrick will be wondering what's happened to me.'

'You're not going back to Patrick? You can't. You mustn't.'

'Why not?'

'You said yourself he's more of a murderer than I am.'

'You didn't agree with me.'

'But don't you see that although I may be the murderer in my own eyes, Patrick must still be one in yours.'

'What do you expect me to do?'

'You can stay here as long as you like.'

'I can't do that,' said Nicholas. He got up from the chair determined to go.

Christopher stared at him in amazement. His expression slowly changed to one of utter melancholy.

He's going to cry again, thought Nicholas. Oh my God, I can't bear it.

Christopher spoke slowly and with difficulty. 'Nicholas, you must listen to me. You're an intelligent person. You've a mind of your own. You mustn't sell it. That would be a crime for which later you'd never forgive yourself. There continually occur moments in one's life when one has to choose between possessions and integrity. I know I'm very silly. I never make myself clear, which is why people laugh at me. But believe me if you choose possessions today you'll regret it for ever after.'

Nicholas looked round the studio. 'I'll collect Michael's portrait later,' he said. 'That is if you still want me to have it.'

'How can you say such a thing?' said Christopher. 'Oh dear. I should have warned you long ago of the danger.'

Nicholas reached the door and turned. Christopher had collapsed on the divan and was huddled in a pose of extreme dejection with his hands cupped beneath his chin. He was staring at the picture of Michael.

'Goodbye, Nicholas,' he muttered. He heard Nicholas run down the stairs. The door slammed.

'Now I know what corruption means,' he muttered. 'Whosoever shall cause one of these little ones to stumble, it were better for him that a millstone were hung round his neck and he were cast into the depths of the sea. That's the right translation. Not *offend*. But *cause to stumble.*'

Nicholas ran along the street looking for a taxi. Hurry, hurry, hurry, he repeated to himself. Why had he wasted so many valuable hours? Why had he hesitated when he had known that only speed could save him? Why had he run out on Patrick last night for a reason that seemed paltry this morning?

He had no idea of what he was going to say to Patrick. He only knew that he must get to him as soon as possible and throw himself at his feet. He would literally grovel on the floor if that was what Patrick wanted.

When he found a taxi he was out of breath from running. As he was being driven across London he sat forward on the seat cursing at every delay. As the taxi approached traffic lights he prayed that they would change from red to green. He felt like leaning out of the window and shouting at the traffic to get out of his way. Before they reached the block of flats where Patrick lived he handed the driver a note. He was out of the door before the taxi had stopped.

As he ran across the pavement he saw Patrick's Rolls drawn up against the kerb. He paused, straightened his tie, and walked quickly through the swing doors.

'Would you ring 108?' he asked the porter.

The porter walked slowly to his desk and picked up the telephone. 'He's arrived, sir,' he said. He replaced the receiver.

So Patrick's not going to see me, thought Nicholas. I've arrived too late.

'You can go up,' said the porter.

As the lift carried him up, Nicholas's spirits started to rise. Perhaps he had been right when he had supposed that Patrick had been as worried as himself. Perhaps nothing mattered to Patrick except that he had come back to him. There might be no need to explain or to grovel. If Patrick didn't care about him he wouldn't have told the porter that he could come up. Patrick was probably waiting in the flat, longing for the moment when the bell would ring.

Nicholas left the lift and walked slowly along the corridor. He did not want to look as if he'd been running.

He paused in front of the door, took out his comb, and ran it through his hair. He deliberately flicked a few strands down over his right eye. That was how Patrick liked it.

Nicholas pressed the bell and waited. He heard Patrick come out of the sitting-room into the hall.

When the door was opened by a strange man his first reaction was to think that in his hurry he had come to the wrong door.

'You'd better come in,' said the young man. 'He's busy packing at the moment.'

Nicholas stepped into the hall. It was stacked with boxes and cases. Through the open door of the sitting-room he saw a large cabin trunk lying in the centre of the room. He turned towards the door of Patrick's room, and saw Patrick standing there smiling at him.

'Well, well,' said Patrick. 'How are you, my dear? It seems such a long time since we met.'

'Patrick . . .' he began.

'How rude of me,' said Patrick. 'You two don't know one another. This is Victor. Victor, this is Mr Milestone.'

Nicholas studied the young man for the first time. He was tall, fair haired with a slightly sallow complexion. Nicholas wondered who he could be and how long he was going to stay. Now that he had got into the flat he had to speak to Patrick alone as quickly as possible.

'I want to talk to you, Patrick,' he said.

'How kind of you. Oh Victor, would you see if you could shut the case in my bedroom.' He turned to Nicholas. 'My dear, come in and sit down. You look terribly hot.'

Nicholas followed him into the sitting-room.

'Isn't packing a bore?' said Patrick. 'The funny thing is that if anyone else does it for you, there's always something left out. The only safe thing is to do it oneself.'

Nicholas was about to close the door.

'No, no. Leave it open,' said Patrick. 'I'm sure I shall have some-thing important to call out to Victor. He couldn't hear if you closed the door, could he?'

So that was who Victor was, thought Nicholas. Some kind of

servant or secretary who had come to help Patrick with his packing. The sooner he went away the better. It was impossible to talk
to Patrick as long as he was about.

'Did you have a gay night, my dear?' asked Patrick.

'Ghastly, Patrick. I stayed in an hotel near Victoria.'

'What a strange thing to do!'

'Don't you see . . . ?'

'I'm sure you'd have been much more comfortable at the
Rialto. I can't think why you've taken against it. It's really the only
hotel.'

'I quite agree,' said Nicholas.

He was beginning to feel secure. It was not turning out as
badly as he had feared. No doubt the storm would break as soon
as they were alone. Meanwhile he must do everything possible to
re-establish himself.

With a sigh of relief Nicholas gazed round the room at the
pictures, bottles, books, the deep armchair and the inviting sofa.
What a difference from Christopher's hovel! He couldn't think
why he hadn't appreciated it more before. It had been ridiculous
of him to think of it as a cell.

'What a lot of luggage!' he said.

'If one's going away for a long time one needs a lot,' said Patrick.
'Victor, by the way, has been kind enough to pack your *things*. He's
put them in the hall. Remember to thank him, my dear.'

'Where are we going?'

'*We?* I didn't know you were coming too, my dear.'

'Of course I'm coming. I've wanted to come the whole time.'

'Then you'd better run along and buy your tickets.'

Nicholas laughed. 'Don't be silly, Patrick. I know perfectly well
you've already bought them.'

Patrick said: 'Naturally, my dear. Why should I be so silly as to
try to travel without them? Do you want to examine them? Perhaps you want to play ticket man and punch holes in them.' He
put his hand in his pocket and took out a folder of tickets. 'There
you are, my dear. Now these are mine. And these are my secretary's. Rather democratic, don't you think? Both the same class.'

'Secretary?' said Nicholas.

'Yes, my dear. What *is* the matter with you? Dear, devoted Victor.'

Nicholas looked at the tickets. 'They're for Bermuda!' he exclaimed.

'Isn't that strange? That's where we're going,' said Patrick.

He was watching Nicholas closely. He didn't take his eyes off him. 'Are you feeling all right, my dear?' he said quietly. 'You've gone the most unattractive shade of green. What about a glass of water? I'm afraid I've locked up all the more delicious drinks.'

Nicholas knew that it was time to go. There was nothing for him to say.

'Where are my things? I'll take them now,' he said.

'There's no need to rush off, my dear. Won't you stay and have some tea? It's such fun picnicking among suitcases.'

'When are you coming back?'

'I've no idea, my dear. A year, two years, perhaps even three. It depends how long I can keep boredom at bay.'

Nicholas walked into the hall. Beside his suitcase he saw a box in which had been packed all the parcels he had bought the day before. He put his hand into his pocket, took out his cigarette case, and lit a cigarette. Through the open door of Patrick's bedroom he saw Victor watching him.

He did not return to the sitting-room. He picked up his case, and slipped quietly out into the passage.

The case was heavy. When he had walked a hundred yards along the street he stopped and called a taxi.

'Where to?'

'Chelsea Square,' said Nicholas.

Patrick did not hear Nicholas go. When he went into the hall and saw that he had been cheated of his final sally he was slightly disappointed. He sighed. How strange to think that only a week ago he had been about to embark upon a new affair with a young intelligent boy. Poor Nicholas! Somehow he had failed to grasp what was expected of him.

Victor came into the hall.

'Was that your nephew, Pat?' he asked.

'No, my dear. Whatever made you think that?'

'His case was just like the one you bought from me six weeks ago for your nephew,' said Victor.

Of course that was the disadvantage of a jeweller's assistant. He knew far too much. Still, he was a novelty. He should be very easy to polish.

'By the way, my dear,' he said, '*Patrick* is my name. I've avoided Pat all my life so I don't think we ought to start now, do you? Now come and sit by me so that I can have a good look at you.'

Patrick examined his hair. A pretty blond colour, but scurfy. Now what was the name of those hair treatment people?

He put out his hand and stroked Victor's hair.

'Patrick! You are wicked,' said Victor.

And those teeth! They must be seen to at once. What was the name of that man in Zürich?

ALSO AVAILABLE FROM VALANCOURT BOOKS

Michael Arlen	Hell! said the Duchess
R. C. Ashby (Ruby Ferguson)	He Arrived at Dusk
Frank Baker	The Birds
Walter Baxter	Look Down in Mercy
Charles Beaumont	The Hunger and Other Stories
David Benedictus	The Fourth of June
Paul Binding	Harmonica's Bridegroom
Charles Birkin	The Smell of Evil
John Blackburn	A Scent of New-Mown Hay
	Broken Boy
	Blue Octavo
	The Flame and the Wind
	Nothing but the Night
	Bury Him Darkly
	The Household Traitors
	The Face of the Lion
	A Beastly Business
Thomas Blackburn	A Clip of Steel
	The Feast of the Wolf
John Braine	Room at the Top
	The Vodi
Jack Cady	The Well
Michael Campbell	Lord Dismiss Us
R. Chetwynd-Hayes	The Monster Club
Basil Copper	The Great White Space
	Necropolis
Hunter Davies	Body Charge
Jennifer Dawson	The Ha-Ha
Barry England	Figures in a Landscape
Ronald Fraser	Flower Phantoms
Gillian Freeman	The Liberty Man
	The Leather Boys
	The Leader
Stephen Gilbert	The Landslide
	Bombardier
	Monkeyface
	The Burnaby Experiments
	Ratman's Notebooks

PETER PRINCE	Play Things
PIERS PAUL READ	Monk Dawson
FORREST REID	Following Darkness
	The Spring Song
	Brian Westby
	The Tom Barber Trilogy
	Denis Bracknel
GEORGE SIMS	Sleep No More
	The Last Best Friend
ANDREW SINCLAIR	The Facts in the Case of E.A. Poe
	The Raker
COLIN SPENCER	Panic
DAVID STOREY	Radcliffe
	Pasmore
	Saville
MICHAEL TALBOT	The Delicate Dependency
RUSSELL THORNDIKE	The Slype
	The Master of the Macabre
JOHN TREVENA	Sleeping Waters
JOHN WAIN	Hurry on Down
	The Smaller Sky
	Strike the Father Dead
	A Winter in the Hills
KEITH WATERHOUSE	There is a Happy Land
	Billy Liar
COLIN WILSON	Ritual in the Dark
	Man Without a Shadow
	The World of Violence
	The Philosopher's Stone
	The God of the Labyrinth

FOR MORE INFORMATION AND A COMPLETE LIST OF TITLES, PLEASE VISIT
OUR WEBSITE AT WWW.VALANCOURTBOOKS.COM

Printed in April 2022
by Rotomail Italia S.p.A., Vignate (MI) - Italy